The Native

BOOKS BY DAVID PLANTE

The Native 1988

The Catholic 1986

The Foreigner 1984

Difficult Women 1983

The Woods 1982

The Country 1981

The Family 1979

Figures in Bright Air 1976

The Darkness of the Body 1975

Relatives 1975

Slides 1971

The Ghost of Henry James 1971

The Native

&

DAVID PLANTE

ATHENEUM
NEW YORK 1988

This is a work of fiction. Any references to historical events; to real people, living or dead; or to real locales are intended only to give the fiction a setting in historical reality. Other names, characters, and incidents either are the product of the author's imagination or are used fictitiously, and their resemblance, if any, to real-life counterparts is entirely coincidental.

Atheneum
Macmillan Publishing Company
866 Third Avenue, New York, N.Y. 10022

Library of Congress Cataloging-in-Publication Data

Plante, David.
The native.

I. Title.
PS3566.L257N38 1988 813'.54 87-33498
ISBN 0-689-11951-8

10 9 8 7 6 5 4 3 2 1

Printed in the United States of America

Part One

&

He opened the bathroom door and saw his daughter's head go under water. When he reached in, up to his elbows, to grab her arms, air rose to the overflowing surface. In anger, he lifted her body out. She was breathing, and he was sure that she let her arms and legs dangle heavily so they would knock against the side of the tub when he pulled her over. He threw her face-down onto the floor and the impact made her cough. He got her to her knees. Her long hair was stuck to her face, naked shoulders and back. She kept coughing.

He shouted, "You were just waiting for me to come in. I know."

She began to cry.

"Get on your feet," he shouted. "Come on, get on your feet."

"I can't," she gasped.

"You can't? You can't?" He took hold of her hair. "You want to kill yourself, really kill yourself? I'll show you how, I'll help you." She clutched the edge of the bathtub as he swung her head by her hair. Bits of toilet paper and cotton balls smeared with make-up were floating on the watery floor. "I'll show you how it's done if you're serious." Her head in his hands, he shoved it down to the water. "I hate, I hate, I hate a faker."

"No," she howled, "no."

He pressed his daughter's face closer to the water. Her breasts against the side of the tub, she strained to hold her head up. His wife came in, shut the taps off and turned the handle to release the plug. Wet, Philip was kneeling, his chest against his daughter's back.

"Both of you get up," Jenny said.

Philip let go of Antoinette and stood.

"Help her," Jenny said to him.

His hands slipped on her wet skin. She staggered a little when he took his hands away.

"Stand up," her mother said to her.

Antoinette leaned against the washbasin; her head bent low, her body wobbled.

"Go on," Jenny said to Philip, "leave us alone."

He went to their bedroom, slammed the door, took off his wet clothes, and got into bed. He twisted and turned and kept thinking he should get up and go out to them; but he remained in bed and when, finally, the door opened, he began to shiver. Jenny did not switch on the light. Philip tensed the muscles of his neck, arms, legs to try to stop himself from shivering. Jenny got into bed. He knew he should ask her how Antoinette was, but he couldn't. He knew he shouldn't have an erection. She asked, "How are you?" When he felt his wife's hand on his bare shoulder, he turned towards her. Her body was warm.

Before he fell asleep, he asked, "Where is Toinette?"

"In bed." Then he heard as from a distance. "After you leave tomorrow, I'll take her into Boston, back to the doctor, and ask if he thinks she should –"

In the dimness was a deeply polished, blond-wood dining table with a lace runner, and in the middle an empty milk-glass bowl. Jenny, holding the edge of the table, was looking out of the window, where there was more light than inside the room.

Her husband came in from the kitchen and saw her. He pressed a switch and the lamp hanging over the table lit, a white glass shade fluted about the edge and supported by a brass ring and three brass chains. With a small jerk of her body, she turned to him, smiling, and raised her hands. Behind her was a glass-paned highboy, the wood as light as the table; through the reflections of the lamp on the panes appeared, themselves like transparent reflections, white cups and saucers, and behind these were plates tilted on edge. She always blinked rapidly when she was surprised – or perhaps she wasn't surprised, but wondered why her husband was standing at the door. Her ash-blond hair was short.

Philip said quietly, "You were in the dark."

"I was looking out the window," Jenny said as quietly.

Philip pulled out a chair and sat, turned a little away.

Jenny said, "Isn't it nice that it's Friday?"

"I was thinking, driving home, that I should visit my mother some time over the weekend."

"I'll come with you."

"You don't have to. You know that."

She got up and walked around the table and stood behind him and put her hands on his shoulders; she lowered her chin to the top of his head, on the bald spot.

She said, "Antoinette stopped by today."

"When?"

"Not long before you came in from work."

"She wouldn't wait for me?"

"I told her not to."

"Maybe you're right." He took one of her hands from a shoulder and kissed the palm. "And how was she?"

"I thought she was in a good way. I mean that. I thought she was in a really good way."

She drew her hands away. Philip stood to follow her into the kitchen. He leaned against a counter as she took from the refrigerator a steak in cellophane, unwrapped it and put it on a white plate.

"She bought herself a car," Jenny said.

"A car? I was wondering how she got here. How about that."

"I told you she's better."

"Did she tell you where the money came from?"

"Her job, I suppose."

"She's got a job?"

Jenny nodded and said, "Ah-hun," and held her chin up, blinking rapidly.

"You know," Philip said reflectively, "I wanted her to come home to live after she gave up everything in Boston. I wanted her to think we believed in her when she didn't believe in herself. But she went too far. When she tried to kill herself, I couldn't believe in her any more."

"She knows that after all you did she went too far."

"Does she?"

"She does."

"I couldn't take what she did."

Jenny raised her chin more and pressed her lips together.

"Not like you," he said. "You never stopped believing in her."

"Oh," Jenny said, "there were times when I nearly felt the most reasonable thing would be to let her go, let her go kill herself if that's what she wanted."

"Not really."

"Yes, really. If she hated life so much –"

Philip put his arms around her. "What do you know about hating life?" he asked.

"Only what I've learned from you two."

She leaned away from him to look at him. His face was thin and dark, his fine nose broken and a little askew; his irises were black.

Holding her, he said, "You shouldn't come with me to visit my mother. You honestly shouldn't."

When he made love with her that night, he felt about them both a sense of deep calm that circled them at a dark distance. Perhaps his efforts for that deep calm counted for nothing, and he had to give in to it happening of itself, as he gave in to his love for his wife. Lying awake as she slept, his foot on her leg, he thought: This is not an exaggeration, this is not false.

They drove over a hill on the highway, wet from melted snow, and other hills appeared around them, covered with late winter woods like grey clouds, and here and there a pine tree in those clouds. The sky was clear blue.

Philip said, "Maybe I'll see Toinette tomorrow afternoon."

"She told me she'd be visiting your mother tomorrow afternoon."

"Has she been visiting my mother?" Philip asked.

Jenny raised her chin. It was an answer, her raising her chin, but he never knew what answer.

"Has she?"

"Almost every day," Jenny said.

"My mother hasn't said anything about that to me." Philip frowned. "Their secrets."

Jenny asked him about his work.

Philip turned into a drive between stone walls and parked. On both sides of the lot were snow banks, and, beyond, woods, the bare, thin, grey branches diffused in the heavy sunlight, so the trees seemed to stand in mist. He took Jenny's arm as they walked round the puddles to the stone building, set among the cloudy woods.

In the foyer, to the side of the double glass doors, three old people, two men and a woman, were sitting in the sunlight. The skin of their faces looked as though it were flaking. Outside the block of light, in the rest of the foyer, there seemed to be empty space, but, once in it, Philip saw other old people: a row of them against a wall in wheelchairs, staring out. Down a corridor from the foyer was the nurses' station, and Philip recognized his mother talking to a nurse across the counter, which was almost as high as her chin. He stopped for a moment, Jenny a step behind, to watch his mother as from a long distance, too far to traverse except in memory. Her white hair was chopped short; her dress was too big, her cardigan too small, and she wore large slippers with furry turndowns. A white-haired black man, moving in slow jerks with a walker, was coming from deeper down the corridor, and Philip's mother shuffled to him to take his arm and guide him to the counter, talking all the while. She continued to talk to the nurse without stopping, her hand still at the black man's elbow, as if he needed someone to talk for him. He wore a green plaid flannel shirt, open on a white undershirt, and baggy trousers. The nurse tried to communicate directly with him, but Philip's mother talked for him while he looked at the nurse with a stern face, his jaw a little twisted. The nurse said, "Reena, let him tell me what he wants, he can," but Philip's mother, the wrinkled lips of her round, toothless mouth going in and out, had to say what she had to say before she would be stopped.

Philip went to her. He leaned low and said, "Momma." She turned to him with a little look of fear in her unfocused eyes and said, "But I was only trying to help him." Philip said, "I know," and she raised her hands and exclaimed, in a high, thin voice, "Oh Philip," and grabbed the sleeves of his overcoat in both hands. "It's my son Philip," she said. She looked around at the nurse and the black man, and at others standing in the corridor. "It's my son Philip," she called. He held her arms and drew her to him to kiss her on her cheek. She put her arms around his waist. Her face came up to his abdomen. She pressed her face sideways against him and he saw her skull through the thin, yellow-white hair parted and held flat by bobby pins, her flaking forehead, her long, gaunt nose, and hairs on her pointed chin. Her small body was bony, and smelled of urine. Her eyes, he noted, kept shifting to see if anyone was looking at her in her son's arms.

Every time he came, she greeted him with this show. He came every second week. This time, one week had gone by. Perhaps she would put on the show even if he came every day. He wanted to get her out of the corridor into her room. He felt something like repulsion towards his mother, but he held her, there in public, until she drew back and looked up at him with those half-focused eyes, as if all at once not sure who he was. He was not convinced that she was as blind as she insisted she was.

"I've come with Jenny," he said.

"Who?"

"Jenny."

"Oh, where is she? Where is she?" She shuffled as she turned. He was sure she could, if she wanted, walk normally, but she said she couldn't, and was frightened of falling and breaking her hip. "Where is my beautiful, beautiful, so beautiful daughter-in-law?"

Jenny stepped forward and, stiffly, held her mother-in-law's shoulders and kissed her slack cheek. "Hi, Mem," she said, which was her approximation to Mémère.

Her mother-in-law raised and lowered her head to see, and said, "It's too dark."

"Let's go to your room," Philip said.

"Wait," his mother said. "I just want the nurse to –" She shuffled round again. "Nurse," she said.

The nurse, with a slight smile at Philip, asked, "What is it now, Reena?"

"Did you meet my son?"

"I did, yes. I met him many times before."

Philip nodded at her.

"And my daughter-in-law?"

"Yes. I did."

Philip said to the nurse, "I guess she likes acting up."

"Oh, we know Reena," the nurse answered in a singsong, "we know about her acting up."

Philip's mother shuffled between him and Jenny down the corridor, and stopped at every person they passed. She patted the heads of those sitting in wheelchairs, and she patted the hands of those standing against the wall. She kissed the cheek of an old man who turned away as she kissed him.

"Don't you want to meet them?" she asked Philip.

"I've met them," he said. "Anyway, I don't think they want to be disturbed."

"Hun?"

"They don't want to be bothered," he answered in a louder voice.

"The nurses tell me that I bother people too much. They've forbidden me to go into anyone else's room but mine. Sometimes they restrain me in my room. I don't like that. I don't like being tied to my chair. They tell me I'm making a pest of myself, always wanting to talk to others. I say, 'All right, I'll stay in the corridor, I'll talk to people in the corridor.'"

She went off at an angle to an old woman, by a doorway, wearing a pink wig, and she took the woman's hands in hers and held them to her bosom. Smiling, the woman leaned close to Reena and whispered, and Reena frowned and bit her lower lip. When she got back to Philip and Jenny, she said, "I'm not going to introduce you to her. I don't want you to hear what she says."

They passed a room in which an old man, naked, was making up his bed.

Philip asked his mother, "How's Arthur?"

"Always unmaking and making his bed," she said, "all day long. Do you want to meet him?"

"He doesn't have any clothes on."

She pressed her lips together.

"Why aren't you wearing your false teeth?" Philip asked.

"I lost them."

"You lost them? Where?"

"Somewhere. My room mate said I was wearing hers. I wondered why they didn't fit. I gave them back to her, but I couldn't find mine."

"You should get a new set."

"No, it doesn't matter. I'll be dead soon. It doesn't matter."

"Momma," Philip said as a reprimand.

Jenny said, "That's a pretty dress you've got on, Mem."

Reena smiled. "Oh, thank you."

Over his mother's head, Philip looked at his wife and winced.

"I've never seen it before."

"No. I don't know where it comes from. All our clothes get mixed up in the laundry. That doesn't matter."

"It's pretty, whosever it is."

"I never noticed it."

"Honestly, it is pretty."

Her mother-in-law laughed, a kind of squeal. "I think you're lying to me."

Jenny raised her chin.

As if there were a wide, deep space at the threshold of her room, Reena, holding the door jamb, lifted a foot as high as she could to step over and in.

Philip thought it was his fault that his mother had to live in this room, that she couldn't find her teeth, that she wore other people's clothes, that, too, she wore a clear plastic identification band around her wrist with her name and blood type on it. At the same time, he felt it wasn't his fault, it was her fault.

She didn't have to be there. Her helplessness was, he felt deeply, a pretence.

Pretence? he thought. Oh no.

Her back widow-humped, she shuffled in the light which streamed through the window towards an old woman with long, white hair, who was tied into a chair, asleep, her head sunk far to one side.

This woman was wearing a loose hospital gown, and her feet were bare. Reena, her body bent forward, bent even further forward to take the old woman's feet in her hands, and she asked, in her old French, *"As tu frette, Mama Culotte?"* but the old woman remained asleep. "She gets cold," Philip's mother said to him. "I've got to find socks to put on her."

"Maybe she doesn't want socks put on," Philip said.

Her arms crossed at her waist, Jenny stood at the back of the room.

Reena shuffled to a built-in dresser. On the wall over it was taped a child's drawing of a house and a tree and a beaming sun. In a drawer filled with tangled clothes, Reena found two mismatched socks and made her slow way, arms outstretched a little to keep her balance, back to Mama Culotte, but she couldn't manage to pull the socks over the almost club feet.

Philip asked, "Do you want help?" but he knew he wouldn't be able to touch the old woman.

"She's cold. I know she's cold. Feel her feet."

Jenny said, "I'll help you," and came to take the socks from her mother-in-law's hands.

Mama Culotte woke up as Jenny was putting on a sock, and, lifting her head just enough to see what was happening, she kicked out with one foot. Shocked, Jenny stood back. Mama Culotte closed her eyes and dropped her head to the side again. Perhaps she hadn't been asleep.

"I told you she didn't want to be bothered," Philip said to his mother.

"But she's cold. I know she is."

Blushing, Jenny held the two dangling socks for a moment before she put them back in the drawer and closed it.

"Everything I do is wrong," Reena said. "Everything."

"Come on, Mem," Jenny said, "let's sit for a while and chat."

"If that's what you want, I'll do what you want."

Jenny helped her mother-in-law to the green plastic upholstered chair in the sunlight, where she talked as if she had been talking in the same way for hours, for days and for years, without end.

"I know, I know how you want me to be. I know you want me to be well and happy. And I do my best. I do. I do. I do it for you. I make efforts. You don't know what I suffer having to make the efforts. You can never know. But I do it. I can't sleep and I lie awake, but I don't ring for the night nurse. I say to myself, Just lie awake, just bear it. I do. Ah, and if you knew what I bear, what I've had to bear, but you won't ever know, ever –" Her little, toothless mouth opened and contracted rapidly like a – Philip thought, he didn't want to think what it was like – and she paused only long enough to stick her wet, pointed tongue out of the soft, wrinkled, wet orifice. "And when I have to take my shower in the morning, and the water is cold, I say to myself, 'Don't complain,' though I'm shivering. Everyone tells me, 'Don't complain, don't complain,' everyone tells me what to do, but I, I can never tell anyone else what to do, because everything I want is wrong, even if all I want to do is help someone who's cold. But I grit my teeth –" Here she exposed her bare gums and clenched them together. "I bear it. I bear everything –"

Still in his overcoat, Philip sat back in his chair and put his left hand to his forehead. He felt that all his muscles were loose, and he was not sure he had the strength to get up. He turned the hand at his forehead so he could look at his watch and saw he hadn't been with his mother for more than twenty minutes, and he must stay for at least an hour.

Jenny interrupted her. "It's a nice day out, Mem. Wouldn't you like a walk outside around the grounds? It's really a nice day."

"A walk outside?"

"I'll help you get your coat and boots on."

"There's snow outside."

"It's all melted."

"Then there'll be water."

"With boots on, we can walk through the puddles."

"No, I don't want to go out."

Jenny stood. "I think you should. You're always inside."

"No."

"Come on, Mem. It'll do you good." When Jenny stood against the light, she appeared large. "Come on."

If Jenny had been a Catholic, her mother-in-law would have known how to deal with her; but because she was a Protestant and therefore, even after so many years in the family, a kind of foreigner, Reena was unsure of herself, and she looked at Jenny with shifting eyes.

"If you want me to," Reena said.

Unable to move, Philip watched Jenny help his mother put on stockings, boots, coat, scarf, hat, mittens. This took almost half an hour. All the while his mother talked, he was not quite sure about what. And she talked while they went round the parking lot, slow step by slow step, he holding one of his mother's arms, Jenny the other. Philip heard only phrases.

"– that was because I couldn't, and they said I could, but I knew I couldn't – so I said, I said, 'Just let me be' – because it doesn't matter –"

All of this she said in a dry whisper, flatly.

"Just let me die."

He wanted to say to her, sharply, as he had heard his father say sharply to her, "Stop it. You're only doing this to get attention, you know that. Stop it."

Oh Christ, he thought, oh Christ.

"I'm tired," she said. "I want to go back to my room."

"Don't you feel better for taking a little walk?" Jenny asked her.

She shrugged. "Yes. Maybe. I don't know."

Her son and her daughter-in-law had to help her, a step at a time, up to the entrance.

Inside the foyer, she said, "Leave me now. I'll go back to my room on my own."

"But can you get undressed?" Jenny asked.

"I'll do it, somehow."

"We'll help you," Philip said.

"No," she said. "Go on."

"If that's what you want."

"That's what I want."

He held her and when he kissed her, he closed his eyes. Then Jenny kissed her.

She said to Jenny, "I didn't want to go out for a walk."

She turned and left them, her boots squeaking. The other inmates were ranked along the sides of the corridor. Philip saw his mother go towards a man sunk low in a wheelchair. She talked to him as she approached him. Philip thought that he looked like his father just before he died.

He said to Jenny, "Why do I feel she has the will to help herself if she wanted to?"

"The doctors said she needed to be here."

"Yes, I know. But I still feel –"

He watched her hold the old man's head in her mittens and kiss it.

He thought that they would come back again and again, these images of her. They would strike him with the force of images of a world unable to help itself, and at these striking moments the images would overwhelm him.

Philip was from the North. He had met Jenny in Texas. He was invited by a friend from Otis Air Force Base, where they were both stationed, to spend the weekend with his family on their cotton farm near the Gulf. His friend George got tickets for a football game; he had a date, and he fixed up Philip with his sister Jenny. The football players' uniforms were wet with sweat in the hot, humid air. Walking across the parking lot after the game, side by side, ten paces behind George and his date, Philip and Jenny were silent. Perhaps it was because he had only brothers that Philip didn't know how to talk to a girl. Jenny reached out and took his hand.

Talking with his mother about his future marriage when he was back in the North on leave, he said, "I know I'll never argue with my wife."

They were in the kitchen, at the table, drinking tea.

"Tell me that again in thirty years," she said.

"I know I won't."

"You don't know."

He was leaning back and rocking on the rear legs of the chair. "I'm sure all you have to do is make up your mind not to."

"Supposing your wife said that you were ruining the chair by sitting in it that way?"

Philip sat forward. "I'd say, 'You're right,' because she would be right."

"Right has nothing to do with it."

"A marriage can be thought out."

"No," his mother said, "it can't."

Philip's younger brother Daniel, who was about thirteen, came into the kitchen carrying a book. He held it out to Philip and his mother with outstretched arms and asked in a high voice, "How did this book get into the house?"

"What is it?" his mother asked.

"A Protestant bible. I found it in the attic."

"Let me see it," Philip said.

Daniel pulled it to his chest.

"I don't know how it got into the house," his mother said.

In a clear, controlled voice, Philip said, "In this house, we live hundreds of years back."

"Oh I –" his mother began.

Daniel went to the kitchen door, opened it, and threw the bible down the cellar steps.

"What are you doing?" his mother asked.

"Get that book," Philip said.

"No," his brother said.

"Go get it."

"No."

Philip went. He carried the bible up the worn, wooden steps, smoothing out the pages. The bible had a green cover, a silver top edge stain and a red thumb index.

Daniel said, "You're committing a sin, saving that book."

"Stop it," Philip said, and returned to his chair at the kitchen table.

"It's the devil's book."

Frowning, his mother said to Daniel, "Let us be now. We were talking."

He left, and Philip said to his mother, "How can I bring my wife into this house?"

His mother frowned more.

Philip put the bible on the kitchen table and went into his room to lie on his bed and think of Jenny in Texas.

While packing to go back to the Air Force base, he recalled the bible. He found his mother in the pantry, peeling potatoes, and he asked her where the bible was. She looked at him for a while with lips pressed together.

As if unable to say more about a terrible but necessary act she had committed in secret, all she said was, "It's gone," and Philip wondered what terrible but necessary acts of will his mother was capable of.

In a low voice, he said, "You shouldn't have done that."

He realized that it was not so much her getting rid of the bible that he could not take, it was that his mother should make up her mind to get rid of it, to be so wilful.

Philip brought his wife Jenny to meet his mother when his father, who disapproved of the marriage, was at work. His mother embraced his wife, pressed her forehead to her daughter-in-law's temple, and wept.

Jenny smiled.

Philip's mother said to her, "We know so little here about the world."

Jenny kept smiling.

"Our ideas are old. It wasn't that Philip's father thought anything bad about you or your religion, it was that he –"

Jenny put her hand on her mother-in-law's arm and said, "I understand."

"Do you?"

"Yes."

"We hardly understand ourselves."

Jenny said, "What a pretty house you have."

Her mother-in-law laughed a little. She knew Jenny was lying, but she liked it that Jenny was lying.

She said, "I asked Philip's father to decorate with all bright colors."

And then she seemed to make an act of will. She hadn't wanted Jenny to see this house, but now that Jenny was in it, Reena deliberately turned her shame round to a kind of unreserved exposure by saying, "I'll show you the house." Maybe she wanted Jenny to see the worst of her family's secret life, and then there would no longer be secrets.

Jenny's look was that of someone who understood what she was seeing, understood in ways Philip and his mother couldn't. Evidently, she didn't find anything strange. Smiling slightly, she looked at what her mother-in-law exposed to her. It seemed to Philip she could, if she'd wanted, have explained to them why they lived in the house they did, in a little French parish in Providence, Rhode Island.

Jenny and her mother-in-law talked of going downtown one day to do shopping together.

After tea, Philip's mother suggested that they all go visit Matante Oenone. Philip felt his mother was going too far in showing Jenny their way of life, and he wondered why she wanted to do this. She didn't like Matante Oenone. She didn't like any of his father's family. She thought Oenone was a backwoods woman, dark with superstitions, and she was in no way curious that those superstitions were partly Indian. She wasn't Indian, and didn't want to know about the Indian ancestry of her husband and sons, however little there was to know about it. She must have known that Matante would, before a non-Catholic, take it upon herself to demonstrate to the full what it was like to be their kind of Catholic.

Matante Oenone showed Jenny around her tenement apartment. Jenny didn't say anything. She only looked. Philip's mother stayed towards the back of the group. As if determined to get a reaction from Jenny, Matante Oenone opened her closet door, pulled open the drawers of her bureau, showing the places where holy pictures most attracted divine attention. The most effective place was behind the headboard of the bed, but as the bed was huge it couldn't be moved, so the presence of the pictures behind it had to be taken on faith. Matante, with her big Indian arms, could have picked up all the furniture in her room at once, but she was aware that as a French lady she must appear delicate, and she had Philip lift a corner of the mattress to reveal pictures spread out on the box spring – another good place for them, because she slept on them, and they had cured her of many illnesses, including cancer. Jenny, Philip saw, was embarrassed. Or, if Jenny wasn't, he was embarrassed, and stepped back to lean against a wall, under a framed oleograph of the Holy Family, when Matante explained to Jenny her daily rituals of prayers before certain especially potent pictures. Philip set his jaw. He didn't want Jenny to see what they believed in his family, and he wanted to take her away. His mother was smiling a little, looking at Jenny.

They sat around the kitchen table. With a passion even greater than her passion when she was speaking of the wounds of Jesus, Matante Oenone described the filthy kitchen of a neighbor and her filthy body, whose skin was like the bark of a tree. Philip hoped his aunt would say that, as an act of charity, she washed the neighbor and the kitchen as well, but, as he'd expected, she only said, "And the Holy Mother of God appeared to that woman."

Philip's mother tried to laugh. "Well, she's appeared to people who're even more funny than that."

"You don't have to be funny for the Holy Mother to appear to you," Matante answered.

Sweat rose to Philip's skin as he imagined listening to the talk from Jenny's position at the other side of the round table.

Matante said, in a low voice, "Just last night, I was in my bedroom undressing to get into bed, and I hadn't taken off my corset when something made me look at the statue of Sainte Anne, there, the very mother of the Mother of God, on my bureau, there, and when I did, it was like the room went dark, went as dark as the darkest night, and the walls and the floor and the ceiling went away, so I was outside, and Sainte Anne, there, slowly raised her arms, looking at me."

The others around the table waited as though for something to happen.

Philip's mother half whispered, "What did she want?"

"She didn't speak, but I know what she wanted," Matante said.

"What?"

Again, Oenone kept a long silence, then said, "I know."

Philip touched Jenny's arm. "Come on," he said, "we'll go."

On the way home through the parish, his mother said to his wife that she didn't at all believe what Oenone had said.

Jenny said, simply, "I guess it'd be hard to."

"Sometimes I feel that I married into a world that didn't have anything to do with mine. Well, for one, I didn't even know that Philip's father was part Indian."

Jenny frowned. "Part Indian?"

Philip laughed, and said, "I didn't tell you."

After a moment, Jenny laughed, too. "Let's not tell anyone in my family," she said. "I don't know if people back home in Texas would like it."

"I refuse to believe what Oenone believes," Philip's mother said. "I refuse to." And then, as if as an appeal, she said to Jenny, "I don't want to live in the dark any more, I want to live where everything is bright."

Before Antoinette was born, Philip and Jenny, in their new home, played a game of Chinese checkers after dinner on a card table in a corner of the living room. He was losing. "I don't know why I'm playing this," he said; "it's a stupid game." She moved another of her white marbles into a hole in a triangle of the star on the board which was almost filled with her white marbles. Philip grabbed the corners of the table and tipped it over, on its side; the board crashed to the floor and the black and white marbles bounced, pinging on the wooden floor, and rolled in all directions. Philip and Jenny sat with the empty space between them.

Jenny said lightly, "Well, we'll never play that game again."

She got up and righted the table, put the board back on it, and began to collect the marbles.

It took him a while to unclench his teeth. "Don't do that," he said, his voice clenched.

"You don't want me to pick things up?"

"No. I don't want you to."

"Oh, in that case, I won't." She threw the marbles up in the air and walked out.

Sprawled on the floor to reach under the couch, he felt his anger rise, but he kept it down. He found all the marbles, and, carrying the board with them trembling in the holes, he went to her in the bedroom.

"Do you want another game?" he asked.

She was lying on the bed, reading. "No. I meant it when I said we wouldn't again, and I meant it because I know it's better if we don't."

"Are you angry?"

"No."

"You really aren't."

She said, "It makes me understand you a little more."

"I don't know if there's much to understand."

He believed she understood more than he did. He could explain to her what kind of photographic lens his company was designing, and he could count on her getting the idea. Though he was a little angered that his wife should assume she understood everything, he loved the understanding of his wife. As it seemed to him that the spacious clarity of her mind was due to her being a Protestant, he loved her for being a Protestant and unlike him, a Catholic from the Northern woods – woods where the French immigrants had been for so long they'd developed a closed, dark religion of their own, and had intermarried with the Indians.

Over the thirty years she had lived with Philip in New England, Jenny had lost her Southern accent and come round to liking the hard winters and disliking the soft air of the South, but she never became a Northerner. Though she played the organ at nine o'clock Mass for the Catholic church her husband and daughter attended, she was never converted to Catholicism. He didn't want her to be a Catholic. The furniture of her house, a large, clapboard house outside the town, was of blond, gleaming wood, and the walls, curtains, bedspreads, and some of the rugs, were white.

Philip was splitting logs by the driveway when Antoinette drove up in her old, big car. He couldn't see her through the windscreen, on which, in a long curve, the tops of bare trees, the gables of the house and the deep, grey sky were reflected, but she had said she would be coming at this time in the afternoon. He rested the ax head on the squat log. No one got out of the car. He leaned the ax handle against a tree trunk and stepped towards the car just as the door opened and his daughter got out. Her long skirt furled about her high, black boots as her long hair furled about her shoulders, and he was struck by how beautiful she was, more beautiful than his wife. He took off his gloves as he went to meet her. They stood before one another, and Antoinette said, "Hi," and he answered, "Hello."

She said, "You were making fire wood."

"I thought I'd keep the supply up to a good cord."

'I'll split some, too."

"You can watch."

He put his gloves back on. She stood by the stack, held between two oak trees, while he raised the ax and chopped an upended log in two with one swing. She picked up a half and placed it on the block, and he split this in two. They gathered the splintered quarters and stacked them with the other.

She said, "The time you're putting into cutting logs you could be putting into some other work, and with the money you earn from that you could pay to have the logs split to just the size you like, delivered, and have some money to spare."

"You may have a point." He smiled back at her. "Except that, most likely, I wouldn't be working for myself."

"Working for yourself, you may be losing a lot."

"I may," he said.

Splitting another log, the ax head got stuck in the cleft.

"God damn it," he said. When this happened, he was capable of throwing the ax and the log into the woods. He pressed his lips together. Antoinette held the end of the handle while he hammered the ax head, deeper into the log with a sledge hammer. The clanging gave way to the crack of the log. He split the halves, and she gathered the quarters in her arms and followed him to the garage where he put the ax away. After all the clanging, the silence was high and wide, and filling with snow.

Inside in the darkening den, he took the split log from her, put two pieces in a wooden box, and the other two into the front of the sheet-iron stove and shoved them into the fire with a poker. Antoinette lit a floor lamp.

"Where's Ma?" she asked.

"She went out for a while."

"Where to?"

"I'm not sure." He was hanging their coats on a coat stand. "I guess," he said, "she wanted us to be alone."

"I'd guess that's what she'd want."

Philip remained standing after she sat in an armchair under the lamp.

"Don't you want to take your boots off?" he asked. "They're getting water all over the rug."

"And what about you?"

He lifted a treaded sole to look, and then bent over to untie the heavy shoes. Antoinette pulled off her boots. She placed them with his shoes behind the stove, then sat again, this time on the sofa.

Her head to the side, she said, "Do you know what she wants us to do alone?"

"No."

Antoinette put a finger to her lips. Her long face was dark, and her large, long-lashed eyes were dark. This didn't come from her mother, whose square face was pink, whose narrow eyes were blue; and it came from something deeper than her father, because she was darker than he. She was twenty.

He remained standing.

"I've stopped going to the doctor," she said. "Finally, I wasn't able to talk even with him without feeling that I was putting on some kind of act."

He kept himself from scratching his neck; he didn't have to scratch his neck.

She said, "I've decided it's not bad, this sense that everything you do is silly. Maybe it's even good, like some kind of conscience." Her hand was on her forehead, so her eyes were half hidden. Her lower lip twitched and she said flatly, "And yet, I can't help feeling, can't help thinking, all the time, all the time –" She bit her convulsing lower lip.

Smiling at him, she smeared her tears with her long fingers. Her face shone.

"Do you want a handkerchief?" he asked.

"Yes, please."

There wasn't one in his pocket, he knew. To get away from her for a moment, he went into his bedroom to take a handkerchief from the chest of drawers, then he leaned against the chest.

In the den, he gave the handkerchief to Antoinette, who opened it up and pressed it over her forehead and cheeks and chin, then gathered it together about her nose and blew into it.

Her voice was filled with phlegm. "It's silly, but I can't help it." More tears welled into her eyes. "It's too silly to be real suffering, I know it isn't suffering, unless what I suffer is my silliness, my own stupid silliness." She hit the arms of her chair with loosely clenched fists. "I wish I could be more like Momma."

His face twisted with pain, his hand out to place it on her shoulder, Philip stepped towards her. She looked up at him with a look he'd seen before. When she was a little girl she could will herself to cry. Her eyebrows contracted over the bridge of her nose. It was as if she were all at once angry that something she wanted to go on, to go on and take her over and remove her from the responsibility for her actions, was leaving her to herself, and she didn't like this. She wanted to be helpless. Her forced sob sounded a little like a laugh.

His feelings for her went dead.

She was frowning to keep control over her face, which might express some unexpected, even strange, pleasure she wouldn't want expressed. There were no more tears, but she kept dabbing her face and sniffing.

And how did it happen, he thought, that what had been paining her so deeply had turned into a shallow affectation of pain? What was it that suddenly turned her from a person with a soul to one who had to pretend to suffer to have a soul, as if only suffering gave one a soul? How could he pray to God to return the grace to her, if to have God's grace was to suffer?

Why, he wondered, why must grace be in suffering and not in happiness? Why must the grace be dark, why not bright, when it occurred? And when it did not occur, why shouldn't the pretences be pretences to brightness?

He thought of Jenny. She made efforts to be bright even when, especially when, she obviously felt no brightness in her.

Philip thought, with a sense of isolation in the thought, that he never believed his wife had a soul.

In the lamplight, Antoinette pulled her hair so her head jerked, and she said, "The fact is, I'm hopeless."

He heard himself say, "You're not."

"I am, like Mémère."

His scalp began to tighten with rage. "I hate people who say they're hopeless when they're not."

A corner of her mouth rose in a slight smile. "That's inhuman."

"Is it?"

"You know it is."

"No, I don't."

"It is."

"Then I'm inhuman."

The rage came into her eyes. "We'd better stop talking," she said.

"Right."

She put her hands around her neck then drew them out, so her hair rose and fell evenly. Then she sat back stiffly.

He went into the kitchen. As he was getting a drink of water from the sink, Antoinette came in as if she were living in the house and came in unexpectedly from her room upstairs.

Philip did not ask Antoinette if she had been to the home to see her mémère.

Jenny opened the back door. For a moment, she held the back door open, so snow was blown in on freezing air; then she shut the door and said, "That snow is really falling out there." She pulled off her snowshoes while standing on the mat, took off her coat and scarf and gloves and threw them on a chair, and, in her stockings, went to her husband, kissed him, turned to her daughter, kissed her, and asked, in a high voice and a mock Southern accent, "What're you all up to?" She tilted her head from side to side and blinked.

Philip wanted to say, "No, please, don't –"

It was by stark will that Philip – and perhaps Antoinette – sat in the den with Jenny. Jenny asked Antoinette about her apartment, her job in Boston. Philip remained silent.

Antoinette said, "I've got to go."

Always in that falsetto, Jenny said, "The snow is piling up, you know. Maybe you should stay for the night."

"No, I've got to go."

Jenny stuck out her chin as if to receive a punch, but she smiled. Philip had a small urge to punch her.

He kissed his daughter lightly on the cheek after she put on her boots and anorak, then he waited in the den, by the wood stove, while Jenny spoke a little more with her by the door.

Clasping her hands together at her waist, Jenny said to him after Antoinette had gone, "Well –"

"Well? It didn't go well," he said. "In fact, it went very

badly. I think she thinks I'm the cause of what she's going through."

As he spoke, he felt a certain pleasure he knew he should not feel.

He would get angry if Jenny said everything would be all right, and perhaps she was aware he would get angry, as she said nothing except, "I'll get us some dinner."

"I'm not hungry."

He was very hungry.

"I planned on –"

"No," he said, stopping her.

"Then I'll get something together and eat by myself."

He ate with her, and helped her clear the dining room table.

She seemed to him a totally soulless person.

His brother Albert called from Providence to tell him that their mother had fallen and broken her hip, and was now in the hospital. It was a Saturday afternoon in early February, and Philip was alone. He hung up thinking: Of course she fell.

The unconscious, he thought, didn't exist. People pretended to others not to know what they were doing, but they knew.

Jenny found him in the den.

"What's the matter?" she asked.

He shook his head and raised a corner of his mouth. "My mother's gone and broken her hip.

Jenny sat. "Oh."

"She's been operated on. I said I'd go next weekend. I don't think I could face it just now. Will you let Toinette know, and ask her to go?"

For a moment, Jenny didn't move. While Jenny was dialling, Philip wondered if he should go into the garage and sharpen the ax, because he should be doing something. Back in her chair, Jenny said, "She'll go down tomorrow."

He looked around the den then back at his wife. "Did she ask about me?"

"No."

Jenny raised her chin. Maybe, he thought, she did it simply to see better. He should study her each time she did it to find out if, when she tilted her head, she also looked as if she were bringing someone at a distance into focus. She pursed her lips, too, which almost always went with the raised chin.

Jenny seemed to follow her chin, which directed her upwards from the chair and across the room to Philip. She sat on the side of his chair and put her arm across his shoulders.

"Don't worry about your mother," she said. "Hip operations are easy today. She'll be all right."

He leaned his head against her arm. "I was thinking," he said, "that I wish she would die."

Jenny took her arm away and stood.

"It's cook's night out tonight," she announced. "So it's either warmed up leftovers or a restaurant."

"I'll heat up the leftovers," he said.

During the week, especially in the car driving to work and back home, he thought about his mother in the hospital with less sense of his own helplessness than when she'd been in the old people's institution. He knew this was because she was in the hospital for care he couldn't, and his brothers couldn't, give.

He said to Jenny, in the car on the way to the hospital, "I hope to Christ she doesn't have to go into that old people's institution again."

Jenny didn't answer.

"How did Toinette find her?" he asked.

"She said she's weak but –"

"What?"

"Wilful."

"Yes," Philip said, "she's wilful. The weakest woman in the world has the strongest will."

Jenny looked out of the car window.

"You know, it's just come to me how much Antoinette is like her," Philip said.

"I don't see it," Jenny said.

"What amazes me is that I never saw it before. Together they make up a world I've always wanted to get out of."

"What world?"

"You really don't see it."

"No."

"I always wanted to get out of it. I thought I had when I left home, went to college, went into the Air Force."

She laughed a little. "And?"

"You know what I'm going to say: And when I married you. I thought marrying you, I'd really got away."

"Do you hate Antoinette, then?"

"No. No, I love her, as I love my mother."

"But you wish she could be different."

"I guess I do. I don't know."

"It's not her fault, the way she is. I used to think it was, but now I don't."

"And I'm beginning to think it is. I'm beginning to think that by the slightest effort of her will she could change. What else should she use her powerful will for?"

"That's what you want her to do?"

"That's what I want her to do. I suppose, though, I feel she doesn't want to."

When he gave his mother's name at the hospital reception Philip imagined, for a moment, that he'd be told he couldn't see her – as though she'd been imprisoned. He tried to be nice to the fat warden-receptionist in a tight white nylon dress with a zipper up the front, so she would let him in.

A young man in pajamas and a bathrobe got into the elevator with Philip and Jenny and turned towards the wall.

The wide, metal door to Reena Francoeur's room was open, and Philip saw his brother Albert standing at the foot of a bed. In the bed, his mother looked very small.

There was a plaster on her forehead, near her temple, where she had hurt herself when she fell. She was lying flat, with a bottle of blood hanging over her, attached to her arm by a tube; where the needle of the drip was stuck in her arm was another plaster. She was looking up.

"How is she?" Philip whispered to his brother.

Albert said, "They say she'll be well."

As they looked at her, tears rose into her eyes and ran down her hollow temples into her hair. She appeared very clean. Her teeth were in.

Philip leaned close to her, over the metal rail along the side of the bed. "Momma," he said.

Her eyes slowly focused on him. "Philip," she said calmly.

He kissed her. "I've come with Jenny."

Jenny leaned over her and kissed her.

"It was nice to see Toinette when she came down," she said to her daughter-in-law. "We talked."

"She told me."

"I can't talk, really. My mind and body are gone."

"You talked with her."

"I tried. I told her she should try to understand her father." She swallowed. "Where's Philip?"

"Here," he said.

Philip wondered if he knew his mother any more.

In the next bed was an old woman who looked as if she had just come from an operation. A tube ran from one of her nostrils. Asleep, she was turned sideways on the bed, so the tube was twisted. While Philip glanced at her, she turned over onto her back, opened her eyes and called, "Pete, Pete," then closed her eyes again, and, it seemed to him, died. He went closer to her. She was breathing. The woman shouted, "I love you, I love you," groaned, and went silent.

Reena said, "She was operated on this morning for cancer. She keeps calling for Pete."

"Who is Pete?"

His mother shrugged her narrow, bony shoulders. She frowned as she looked at him.

She said to him, "You should make it up with Toinette."

He felt himself go rigid. He said, "I'm always ready to make up anything with her the moment she wants to."

His mother bit her lower lip, then she said to him, "I want to talk to you."

He thought he saw that crazy look in her eyes, when she seemed to be looking at him and past him at the same time."

"If you want."

"On your own."

He wished his brother Albert would say, "For crying out loud, Philip doesn't want to get into any kind of deep talk with you, it's not that time now, either for you or for him," but he stepped back.

Jenny said, "We'll wait outside in the corridor."

His mother watched them go, that look of seeing them and not seeing them in her eyes. They hunched their shoulders as they went out. She said to Philip, "You think I fell and broke my hip on purpose, don't you?"

He hadn't expected this. He raised his hand, palm outward, fingers extended.

"You think that I felt that you, that all of you, stopped believing I was suffering, and I made myself fall to make you believe me again."

For years, he hadn't heard her voice so clear. Her head didn't move, only her thin, wizened lips over her false teeth. Her voice was like her look, though; it seemed to be addressing him, and not.

"You never believed any of my suffering, did you? You always thought, even at the worst times, that I was putting it on, didn't you? Didn't you?"

He lowered his hand.

"I know. Everyone always thought I was putting it on." She swallowed, and all the long, stretched muscles of her throat convulsed. "I suffered."

"Yes," he said softly.

"But you never believed me." Straining, she lifted her head a little and looked to the side. "Where are the others?"

"Outside the room."

"Why?"

"I'll ask them to come back in."

"No." She frowned. "That's right, I sent them away because I wanted to talk to you." She licked her lips. "Will you give me a drink of water?"

On the table by her bed was a pitcher of water. He filled a paper cup and raised her head so she could sip from it. Her head dropped back onto the pillow and she rolled it from side to side, then, as if she saw him unexpectedly, she stared at him, and beyond him.

"I wanted to tell you –" She rocked her head from side to side. "Oh, I don't know, I don't know –"

Holding the metal rail, he leaned towards her.

She said, "Everything, everything, everything you did made me suffer."

He leaned more against the rail.

"Will you raise my bed?" she asked.

By her pillow was a control switch attached to a flex; he pressed a button to make the top part of the bed go up, and she winced as she rose.

"Too much."

He lowered it.

"Higher," she said.

He raised it to the position it was in before. She turned her face to the side and closed her eyes, and he thought she fell asleep. Her breathing was light; her lids twitched. But as he stepped away, she opened her eyes and, without moving her head, she turned her eyes up to him with a crazy look.

Her voice was low. "Don't go."

He stepped back to the bed.

"I know about your sins," she said.

He felt a presence begin to rise up out of him and, larger than he, condemn him for the very fact of who he was.

He said, "Do you?"

"You never thought I did, but I do."

"I'd expect a mother to know her son's sins, maybe even those he doesn't know."

"You wanted to marry someone better than I was. You always thought I was an embarrassment. You married someone you thought was better than I was so you'd be better. But you're not."

The hairs of her eyebrows were long and tangled, and under them her eyes were straining to stare at him from a sharp, awkward angle, as if nothing but her eyes could move.

She said, "You made me feel everything I did for you was wrong, everything, everything. You made me feel –" Her lips moved, but no words came, and her eyes closed for a moment, but she opened them as if startled, and she continued to speak. "I was doing it for the wrong reason – and I thought, Well, what's the right reason? – I remember – 'Will you?' I said – What? – no, no, never mind, never mind – You thought it'd be wrong to say yes, I know you did – You thought it was wrong because everyone was watching – And you believe in God, but you don't believe in me –"

She suddenly turned her head and raised it from the pillow and the tendons stood out in her neck as if no skin was there, and her wind pipe and oesophagus were exposed.

"Not to believe me, not to believe me –"

He held the rail with both hands. Her head fell back. There was agony in her eyes. She stiffly raised a thin, bony hand to touch one of his hands. Shocked, he pulled his hands away.

He went the next weekend to see his mother. The plaster was off the cut on her forehead, but all around it the black and blue mark had spread. Her skin was slack over her skull. This time he had come without Jenny, and no one else was in the room. He kissed his mother, who asked,

"Who is it?" though her eyes were wide open. "Philip," he answered. She kept her eyes open as if waiting for him to say more, then she said, quietly, "You came back."

"Yes."

"Is Jenny with you?"

"She's with Toinette."

"Oh."

A nurse entered and Philip had to stand outside the curtain while she did something to his mother inside.

Pulling the curtain back, the nurse said to him, "She's all right."

"She looks very thin."

"She doesn't eat much, but she's really all right."

Alone with his mother, he said to her, "The nurse tells me you're in good shape."

She raised her chin a little.

"I thought maybe you wouldn't come back," she said.

"Well, I did."

"Put your hand on my forehead."

He placed his hand across her forehead for a moment, then smoothed her hair. She fell asleep.

He telephoned his brother Albert often to ask him how she was. "Pretty much the same," Albert said.

"They're keeping her a long time in the hospital," Philip said.

"That's to keep the bed occupied. As long as Medicare is paying for it, they'll keep the bed occupied until they need it for someone else."

The following Saturday he went with Jenny. His mother slept, waking from time to time with little jerks, and for as long as she was awake she talked, as if she'd been talking about the same things in her sleep, about the capitals of the fifty states, a dead neighbor, a shirt that had to have its collar turned.

Close to her, he said, "Momma."

He seemed to be no one she knew.

"It's Philip," he said.

She whispered harshly, "You shouldn't have come back. I'm not good. I never did anything right."

"No," he said.

"Yes."

His chest heaved, and his breath seemed to come into his lungs in a twisted way.

All the harshness went out of her voice and she said calmly, "If it wasn't that, that was, Portland, Oregon, no, what about Vermont, what is it, that? I know, I know –"

Jenny said to him, "Come on."

Wednesday morning, he told Jenny he'd drive down to Rhode Island right from work to visit his mother. Albert was there.

Wincing with pain, she moved her small body from side to side, plucking at the blanket, and saying, over and over, "*Ça fait mal, Maman, ça fait mal.*"

"She doesn't know we're here," Albert said.

The next day, Jenny telephoned him at his office to tell him that his mother had died.

She said, "Albert thinks the wake should be only one afternoon, and then a simple funeral, without organ or singing."

He saw a pit, and he saw his mother thrown into the pit, as if this burial alone would be equal to her death.

At home, Jenny embraced him. His arms loose, he put his forehead against the side of her head and leaned against her, until he knew she would stumble backwards if he let himself go.

She said, "This is a happy death."

He felt her straining to hold him.

"She's better off. She's not unhappy any longer, and so you should be happy." Jenny shook him a little. "You should be happy. You should be."

He asked, "Does Toinette know?"

"I told her."

After supper, he, alone, drove down to Providence, to the family house. He sat in the kitchen with two bachelor brothers, Albert and Edmond. They wondered when their other four brothers would arrive.

Edmond said, "I don't know if I can see her dead. I don't want that last image of her." He buttoned and unbuttoned the large buttons of his sweater.

"Mère and Père," Albert said, "they thought they were bad, they thought that they didn't count –"

Philip said, "Yes."

"Why? They were good. They gave their country seven sons."

Edmond laughed. He said, "I remember the time she –"

But Philip stood. "I've got to go to bed."

As he was leaving them, he asked, "What did she die of?"

"We're not sure," Edmond said.

"She didn't have an autopsy?"

"No. We didn't want her to suffer in death, too."

In the funeral home, his six brothers stood apart from one another, hardly able to face one another, Philip thought. His oldest brother Richard stood with his wife at the back of the parlor, his brothers Albert and Edmond in different corners. His brother André came to him and told him he had to leave, he couldn't, he said, look at his mother. And his younger brothers Daniel and Julien stood still among the visitors, not speaking to anyone. Philip went to his mother's corpse to say a prayer before it, but he was overcome by a sense of impossibility and he had to turn away. As he did he saw his daughter by the table on which the memorial cards were spread out. They looked at one another. She didn't move. His brother Daniel came to take his place and he went to the back of the funeral parlor.

He believed his mother had an abiding soul.

Part Two

&

It first occurred to Antoinette that her mother wasn't Catholic on a visit with her mother to her grandmother in Texas. The three were in the kitchen. Outside was hot and glaring, inside was cool and dim. They were slicing up fruit from trees on the plantation to make a fruit salad. Antoinette's mother and her grandmother were talking about the church her mother went to when she lived at home. What was odd to Antoinette was that she did not think: Mom is different. She thought: I'm different.

Back in New England, every time Antoinette would go to communion with her father, she'd think: Dad and I are different. Antoinette didn't become interested in finding out about her mother's religion. She became more and more devout in her father's.

He took her down to Providence, to his old parish church of Notre Dame de Lourdes, for Sunday Mass. The sermon was in French, and she didn't understand, but she listened. Her father agreed to stay in church after the Mass was over to show her in which confessional he had confessed his sins, before which statue he had said his penance. On the bottom panes of the stained-glass windows were the names of donors, and these were all French names. As Antoinette and her father walked around the church, she looked for the name Francoeur, but she couldn't find it.

After, she and her father went to his father and mother, her pépère and mémère, and had tea and toast. Her pépère was pleased that she liked the parish church, and he told how he remembered it being built. Her mémère didn't seem to understand why she was interested. When her pépère said, "It turned out to be a beautiful church," her mémère, laughing, said, "Not as beautiful as the Irish, Italian or Polish."

Antoinette went to spend weekends with her mémère and pépère, and felt drawn in by something she shouldn't be drawn in by, as if it were wrong, even a little sinful, of her.

After a weekend with her mémère, she'd return home and tell her mother everything she'd done in the parish. As she talked to her mother she'd think she didn't want to go again to stay with her grandmother in the parish, but when the weekend approached, she'd say, "I want to see Mémère."

Every one of her mémère's sons had left the house except for Edmond, who was often out. She said she found the house big and empty, and she liked her granddaughter's company. Antoinette knew she liked her company because she was a girl. Her mémère asked lots of questions about school, about friends, about dresses, as if she had no idea what a teenage girl's life was, and she wanted badly to find out.

She let Antoinette wander wherever she wanted in the house, and Antoinette would go into the cellar, into the attic, into the backs of closets, looking in old boxes and suitcases. Secrets, she supposed, were dark and closed, and she felt that the parish itself was a secret.

Every Mass she went to in the parish church seemed to her to celebrate some secret, and this was not because of the French language, for that became familiar to her, even, with effort, comprehensible. The secret was somewhere in the religion, which was Canuck Catholic, and being Canuck made the religion the religion of this one small brick church, in this small clapboard parish. The secret was that of a God no one else but Canucks knew, not even other Catholics, and certainly not other Christians. It was hidden, not only by them, but probably from them, this secret of the Canucks.

Once she found a box containing things that had belonged to her father before his marriage to her mother: a baseball uniform and cap, his high school year book, college text books, the paddle he had made for his initiation into his college fraternity, old clothes that smelled of metal.

Antoinette's mother listened to her tell what she had found out in Providence. With amazement, she told her mother that her great grandmother Francoeur couldn't read or write, and made shopping lists by drawing potatoes, onions, carrots, and putting marks after them to indicate how many pounds she wanted. She told her mother, with greater amazement, that her great grandmother made a special medicine from sumac berries. With the greatest amazement, she told her that her pépère's grandmother, her great great grandmother, was Blackfoot. Her mother seemed to know all this, and was not amazed. Sometimes Antoinette wished she'd be more interested, but, mostly, she was glad that she wasn't.

The parish was about to disappear. She asked her pépère how many parishioners there'd been when the church was built and how many there were now, if parishioners were still coming from Canada, if any other nationalities – nationalities, because she assumed, as her pépère assumed, that Canuck was a nationality – like the Italians, Poles, Irish ever joined the French parish, and her pépère tried to answer, rhetorically. To him, to talk about the parish was to talk rhetorically, preferably in French, about *les bons vieux temps*. Mémère didn't talk about old or new times, good or bad.

Antoinette wanted, like her father, to have been born at home, in her parents' bed, and not, as she had been, in a hospital. Like her father, she wanted to have been to Midnight Mass at Christmas when the choir sang in French and, after, to have gone to her great grandmother's for *tourtières* and mashed potato pies and *tire* and oranges. (Her mémère had taught her to say, *"On a des oranges ainques à Noël,"* which she said her mother-in-law had said, and which showed how stingy her mother-in-law was, and was an example of what the *vieux temps* were really like when oranges were allowed only at Christmas.) And Antoinette wanted, like her father, to have prayed to God, the God of the parish, in French.

Her father drove her down to the parish for the weekend, Saturday morning or, sometimes, Friday evening. Her mémère's pale face would appear in the kitchen window as her father drew up to the curb. She would want to ask her father to drive back home right away. She always made a big show of hugging and kissing her mémère.

Alone together, they sat at the kitchen table, and over cups of tea they talked. Antoinette talked more intimately with her mémère than she ever did with her mother.

They talked about her parents' marriage, which Antoinette could never have talked about with her mother or even with her father.

Her mémère said, "You know, the nuns in the parish school used to tell us to cross the street to the opposite sidewalk if we were going to pass in front of a Protestant church. They said that Protestants were evil because they had no souls."

"You thought that?"

"No, of course not. I never thought that. But that's what we were told."

"You never knew any Protestants before you met Mom?"

"I did. I had a friend from when I worked as a telephone operator before I got married who was Protestant. Her name was Emma. After I got married, your pépère thought that because she was Protestant, she was better than we were. We were told Protestants were evil, but we knew they were better. They lived on the East Side, they were the doctors and lawyers and mayors. They were much better than we were."

"I wonder if when Dad married Mom he thought she was better."

"Of course she's better. Your dad didn't want to be like

us. I can't blame him. I don't, at all. He was right to marry someone outside our world and to want to start a life outside our world. Who could ever want to live in the parish?"

One afternoon while Antoinette and her grandmother were talking in the kitchen, her mother came in, carrying a pie wrapped in tin foil. Antoinette's grandmother got up quickly to go to her, and as her mother handed her grandmother the pie her grandmother leaned over it to kiss her on the cheek; but when the two women drew back from one another they blushed a little. Antoinette's grandmother was holding the pie, and she seemed not to know what to do with it.

"I felt like dropping in," Antoinette's mother said, then laughed and looked around the kitchen. Her mother just glanced at her, so as not to let Antoinette know why she had come, but Antoinette knew: it was to see how she was.

Antoinette's grandmother put the pie on the table and lifted the foil and said, "I could never make a pie that's so beautiful."

"It's just apple," Antoinette's mother said.

"And you started with peeling the apples, I'll bet."

Antoinette's mother laughed. "I did have to peel them, Mem."

"I mean, I bet they weren't already peeled and sliced and frozen."

"My mother would've telephoned me from Texas and got angry with me if she thought I was using frozen apples."

"Everything fresh."

Antoinette's grandfather came into the kitchen from the living room, then her uncle Ed. The men said the pie was beautiful. "Really beautiful," Antoinette's grandmother said, "and made with fresh apples."

Before she left, Antoinette's mother wandered around the house, as though looking for something. Antoinette followed her. When her mother paused to look at a holy picture of the Sacred Heart across from the broom closet, Antoinette asked herself: Does she think that's strange? Antoinette now took for granted the bottles of Lourdes water on bedside tables, the rosaries hung over bedposts, the scapulars dangling over bureau mirrors. But in her mother's presence these things became odd, odder to her, Antoinette thought, than to her mother. When her uncle Ed unbuttoned his shirt and lifted his undershirt to show, pinned to it so it lay next to his heart, a frayed bit of green cloth that was a scapular, Antoinette wondered: What do these religious things mean? This wasn't a question she imagined her mother asking, because, really, her mother, she was sure, wasn't interested.

She went out to the car with her mother. Before her mother opened the car door, she turned to Antoinette and asked, "Are you all right?"

Frowning a little, Antoinette answered, "Why shouldn't I be?"

Her mother put her hand on her head.

She asked her father, not her mother, if she could spend the summer with her mémère at the lake house. She was sixteen. Her father looked at her mother, who looked the other way. "Yes," he said, and smiled a little, maybe pleased that his daughter was so attached to his mother.

At the lake, Antoinette and her grandmother would go swimming alone in the still water, then lie on a blanket under the pine trees and talk until her pépère and uncle Ed came home from work. They would lie under the big pines, the branches high up moving a little in a breeze the grandmother and granddaughter below didn't feel, and the grandmother would talk in a way that sounded close to silence. "You say to yourself, This isn't where I want to be, I want to be somewhere else, but you know you've got to stay where you are –"

Antoinette thought about her mother all the while she listened to her mémère.

Her mémère, looking up into the branches, stopped talking, and Antoinette, with the release of being able to say what she could never have revealed to her mother, said, "You wish for what you know you'll never get." As soon as she said this, she blushed.

Her grandmother rolled her head towards her and said, "You're like me," and Antoinette felt a little pull as of someone pulling her back, and she thought, I'm not, not really. She got up and wandered away from her grandmother, whom she looked back at from the path down to the lake. I'm not like her, Antoinette thought. Her grandmother was lying on the blanket. Antoinette went down to the shore and into the lake where she swam quietly in the sunlit water.

While she was taking a walk along the dirt road one Saturday morning, she saw her parents' car through the trees. She waited for the car to stop. She was on her mother's side. Her mother leaned her head out of the window and Antoinette kissed her.

"You've got so dark," her mother said.

Antoinette tapped her open mouth with her hand and said, "Wo-wo-oo," and her father, looking at her past her mother, laughed. He drove the car slowly so Antoinette walked by it as they approached the house.

Antoinette's grandparents came out of the screened porch to greet them. As her father hugged and kissed her grandmother, Antoinette had a strange feeling: she didn't like her father to hug and kiss her grandmother in front of her mother.

Her mother took her grandmother's arm and went off with her towards the blanket that lay rumpled, in mixed sunlight and shadow, under the pine trees. Antoinette didn't follow, but watched them. They didn't sit on the blanket, but walked past, then stood in the full sunlight and talked. Antoinette's mémère laughed at something her mother said.

Antoinette helped her father take little valises and Sunday clothes out of the car. Her parents were going to spend the weekend. Her uncle Ed appeared, and he, too, helped.

He also got the charcoal in the grill lighted for the hamburgers, cooked them, and served them on paper plates to the others who sat around the wooden table on the moss- and weed-grown lawn before the house. A motorboat was speeding over the lake, its bow going thump-thump against the water.

Antoinette's grandmother said to her mother, "I've got a story I've been saving to tell you."

"I'm listening," Antoinette's mother said, and blinked a lot.

"Now, I should tell you, it's a dirty story."

"Mem!"

"Well, we're grown up, aren't we?"

"You are, but I'm not sure about myself."

"Listen." Antoinette's grandmother held her hands up to the sides of her mouth and whispered. "It's a story about a girl who fell into a mud puddle."

Antoinette's mother laughed out. She said, "Oh, Mem, you're so funny."

"That's a joke we used to play on one another when we were kids."

"You really are funny, Mem."

Antoinette's grandmother looked very pleased. She said, "I'd like to be funny."

While her grandparents, and her father as well, were napping, Antoinette sat with her mother on a fallen tree trunk by the woods. Her mother asked her if she was having a good time.

"Yes," Antoinette said, "a great time."

Did her mother look a little worried? "You're not lonely for your friends?"

"No," Antoinette said, "I'm not."

"You don't see many people here in the country," her mother said.

"It's enough for me to be with mémère."

Then, because she thought she should, Antoinette

asked her mother about her Texan grandmother, and as her mother was telling her, her uncle Ed walked up carrying the statue of the Blessed Virgin. Antoinette's mother asked her what he was going to do. This was the first time she asked her daughter to explain to her what was happening in what she seemed, suddenly, to think was Antoinette's family. "I don't know," Antoinette said. She stood and her mother stood. They went toward the woods, but Antoinette hesitated before going in, her mother at her side. Her mother was waiting for her to go in first. They talked because they didn't want Edmond to think they were sneaking up on him. They stopped when they saw, in a little clearing off the path, Edmond piling up mossy stones to form a grotto. He didn't notice anyone. He hefted a stone slab for the top, but it slipped and the grotto fell apart under it. He said, "Damn." The statue was lying on its side among pine needles and pine cones, clutching a rosary and roses. Antoinette and her mother, now silent, watched Edmond begin again to build the grotto beside the heap of fallen stones. When her mother turned away, Antoinette followed her, and they left the woods. Her mother didn't ask her anything. Antoinette asked more about Texas.

She realized that what her uncle Edmond was doing had nothing to do with her mother's America.

After a while, Edmond came out of the woods with the statue and put it back where it had been on a high corner shelf in the kitchen. Antoinette presumed the grotto kept collapsing under the capping stone.

Her parents left on Sunday evening. Antoinette wanted to talk to her grandmother about her mother and father and why her pépère was against their marriage.

Her mémère said, "I think your pépère would have objected just as much to your dad marrying anyone outside the parish. He wanted his sons to marry girls who'd never want to leave the parish. He never wants to leave, and he thought his sons shouldn't either."

"And he wouldn't let you leave?"

Her mémère laughed. "Where would I go?"

She understood her mémère wanting to leave, but, at the same time, she resented her wanting to.

Her mémère said, "I'd never go live with a married son, and his wife. Never." Then her mémère told her how her pépère's side were real Canucks, who led lives which were as close as possible to death.

"His mother used to say that she would never want to come back to life after she died, because we work to die. And I've got to live with that belief."

This belief was, Antoinette felt, her own as well.

At seventeen Antoinette went to college in Boston.

She called herself a Canuck whenever she was asked her nationality.

Her first weekend, she went home and sat up late with her mother to tell her everything that had happened at college the past week. Her father had work to do in his office in the basement.

"Have you made friends?" her mother asked.

"I will," Antoinette answered. "I've met so many people. I know some of them will become friends." She said this because she did not want to disappoint her mother.

Only when she was about to go up to her room to bed did she say to her mother, "I was thinking of going to Providence to spend next weekend with Mémère."

Her mother's chin rose as thought she were putting it out to be hit. "If you want," she said.

Most Friday nights, Antoinette took the train from Boston to Providence.

Her grandmother said, every time, "Your mother will want to see you. Don't you think you should go to see her more often?"

"She's glad I come here," Antoinette said.

"Is she?"

On a snowy, early November Saturday, when her mémère and she were sitting by the radiator in the kitchen for the heat, her mémère put a hand on one of Antoinette's and said, "You're thinking."

Antoinette smiled at her.

"I'm not sure it's good for you to come here," her mémère said.

"Please don't tell me I can't."

"I'd never do that." Her mémère asked, "Tell me what's wrong."

"I don't know."

Her mémère took her hand away from her granddaughter's.

Antoinette said, "I feel the life I'm leading outside isn't my life."

Her mémère said, "It is. You've got to make it yours."

"Can I?"

"I never could. You can, though. You're young and intelligent and educated, and so much more that I'm not. You can do it."

"I believe I've got to," Antoinette said. "But I can't help thinking it's a belief I make myself have. And all the while there's another, stronger belief, and that is in –"

Her mémère said, "We'll take a walk in the snow. We'll go down to the junction and have a cup of tea at the drug store."

When they got back from the walk, Antoinette's grandmother telephoned her mother without telling her she was going to. From the kitchen, she heard her grandmother, in the living room, talk in a way that could have only been to her mother. When she called her, Antoinette went into the living room. Her grandmother held the receiver out.

"Tell your mother to come and spend next weekend with us."

Her mother said to her over the telephone, "Long time no see."

"Why don't you come here next weekend, and we'll be together, the three of us?"

"Which three?"

"Mémère, you, me."

"Would you like that?"

"I'd love it," Antoinette said.

Her mother came, and in front of Antoinette's pépère, almost defying him, her mother said to her mémère, "Let's go downtown to do some shopping. We'll have lunch there. Philip's given me enough money."

Glancing at her grandfather, Antoinette's grandmother said, "It'd be nice to get out of the house."

Antoinette went with her mother and grandmother by bus into downtown Providence. They stayed until the shops, which her mémère called exclusive and which she'd never have gone into on her own, closed. They laughed, trying on clothes, hats, shoes.

Antoinette's mother said, "Let's go to a movie and have supper out."

Her grandmother's eyes widened, but she said after a moment, "No, I've got to go back to prepare supper."

"Pépère and Edmond can prepare. You and Antoinette and I will eat out."

"But they need me."

"For what? They can cook for themselves."

"Yes."

"They can take care of themselves."

"Yes, they can. When I'm not well, they do."

"Why do you have to go back to them?"

Antoinette said, "Come on, Mémère, stay with us," but she knew her grandmother would go home.

Antoinette and her mother shared a bed in a room that had been an uncle's before he left the house; it still had some of his old clothes hanging in the closet which had that metallic smell Antoinette thought of as a family smell. In bed, they talked. Her mother talked about Antoinette's home town outside Boston, as if to remind her of it. She told Antoinette about the latest basketball game she'd been to in Boston or the opera she'd heard on a radio broadcast from New York. Falling asleep, Antoinette held her mother, and she thought: What are we doing in this strange house? Her mother's presence made her aware how lonely, and, in some way, frightened, she was in this house on her own, and she told herself she wouldn't come down the next weekend, but stay with her mother at home. In bed with her, she wanted to tell her mother how much she loved her.

When, in the morning, she told her mother she'd decided not to come to the parish for a while, her mother said, "Well, I'm coming down next weekend. I'm having fun with Mem."

This surprised Antoinette. She thought: Fun with Mémère?

The next Saturday morning, just as her mother and her mémère were about to go out, Antoinette said she did not feel like going downtown. Her mother said, "Then you'll stay here with Pépère." Instead of speaking to her pépère, she went to her room and tried to read.

Her mother and her mémère came home with an overcoat for her mémère which her mother had helped choose. Her mémère put it on. It was yellow with black spots on it and had a velvet collar. Antoinette thought it was ugly, but she said, repeating what her pépère and her uncle Ed said, "Beautiful, really beautiful." Perhaps, she thought, it wasn't ugly, if her mother had chosen it, but really beautiful. Her mother went over and adjusted the soft collar, turning it up. Antoinette's mémère was very happy.

Her mother had to go back home that evening, not, she said, because her husband wanted her home, but because she wanted to be with him.

After she left, Antoinette's mémère said, "I think your mom likes me."

They were alone at the kitchen table.

"I'm sure she does," Antoinette said.

Then her mémère, looking straight at her over her steaming cup of tea, asked, "What do you think about that coat?"

Antoinette drank.

Her mémère laughed so much she had to put her cup down. "It's ugly," she said, "isn't it?"

Antoinette laughed too.

Her mémère couldn't stop. Her pépère came in from the living room where he'd been reading the newspaper to find out why she was laughing. "Nothing," she said. "It's nothing." She wouldn't tell him. He went back into the living room.

Antoinette's mémère said to her, "But your mother is wonderful. She's doing so much for me. I think no one has ever done so much for me. She really, really, really is wonderful."

They did appear to have fun together. When they laughed, Antoinette wasn't sure what they were laughing at: the fat woman on the soda fountain stool eating a banana split? They became excited when, at a counter in a department store, they looked over material for curtains which her mother said she would make for her mémère's kitchen windows. At lunch in a Chinese restaurant, they never stopped talking: her mémère's favorite color was pink, her mother's white, her grandmother's favorite name for a girl was Janine-Marie, her mother's favorite name for a boy was James.

With her mother, her mémère brought scented soaps and bath foam, a fluffy cover for the toilet seat, a clothes hamper, and a rack for her own towel.

"I do love her," her mémère would say to Antoinette about her mother, "I do love her so much."

The three women drove up to the house on the lake on a sunny Sunday afternoon. Antoinette went into the damp, cold house for cushions, which she put on the chairs and glider on the screened porch. Her grandmother and her mother sat on the wicker chairs, and Antoinette lay on the glider, one leg hanging over the edge to rock herself. The sunlight, diffused by the screens, warmed the still air that smelled of pine trees. Antoinette closed her eyes. The voices of her grandmother and mother sounded far, then near, then far. She stopped rocking the glider. She heard her grandmother say, "She's asleep." She wondered if she should tell them she wasn't. Perhaps she was, a little. Just as she was about to open her eyes, she heard her grandmother say in a low voice, "She suffers," and Antoinette felt her body go rigid.

She heard her mother laugh.

Her grandmother said, "I understand."

"Well, I don't know if she suffers, Mem," her mother said. "She doesn't have any reason to suffer. She has everything she wants."

Antoinette felt her eyelids twitching, and she imagined they would suddenly open of themselves, and she would not be able to keep them shut.

Her mother said, "At times, I've thought she was putting it on, her being so sad."

"Putting it on?" her grandmother said in a distant voice.

"Well, it can't have any meaning for her, can it? No one thinks that being sad has any meaning. She couldn't possibly want to be sad. She has every reason to be happy. She's got to be putting this sadness on."

"Why?"

"I don't know why, Mem."

For a while, Antoinette wondered if she was in a place where she in fact wasn't, because there was a sound of wind in the trees outside and no sound around her, and she thought that if she opened her eyes she'd be alone, not on the screened porch, but somewhere else.

Her grandmother's voice sounded weak when she asked, "You think she's putting it on?"

"Yes," Antoinette's mother said. "How can she suffer when she has so much?"

Again, Antoinette heard the wind outside. She was beginning to feel cold, but she didn't move. She had no idea what her grandmother and mother were doing. They weren't talking. When her mother touched her, her body jumped. "We should get back to the city," her mother said. Antoinette tried to smile at her as she rose.

Her mother drove. Her grandmother sat by her in the passenger's seat. All the way into the city, she didn't speak. Antoinette opened the car door for her, and as she got out, slowly, she looked at Antoinette and frowned.

Antoinette's mother didn't come into the house, but said in a high voice, "Goodbye, you all," and went on back to her home.

Antoinette said to her grandmother, "I'll help you get supper ready."

They were in the small pantry.

"I can do it," her grandmother said. "All we're having is soup."

She seemed to want to be alone. Antoinette went to her room until her mémère called her to supper.

From college, Antoinette telephoned her mother to ask her if she'd be going to stay with her grandmother the next weekend.

In that high voice her mother had, she said, "I thought I'd spend the weekend with your loving dad." Antoinette knew that her mother would be blushing.

"I was wondering," Antoinette said.

"If you'd like," her mother said, "I can come down for Sunday afternoon."

Antoinette didn't know if she wanted her mother to come or not.

Her mother appeared with a cake on a glass plate. She almost shouted, "Get out the tea cups." Antoinette's pépère and uncle Ed were visiting her great aunt Oenone. The women sat at the kitchen table with cups of tea and a big cake, which had a thick, swirling, marshmallow frosting.

"Cut it, Mem," Antoinette's mother said, and held out the knife, the blade pointing towards her.

The cake was heavy and soggy inside. Antoinette's mother didn't apologize. She just laughed.

When she was leaving, Antoinette's grandmother said

to her, earnestly, "You'll come and stay, won't you? Can't you come to stay next weekend? Please come."

Again, all Antoinette's mother did was laugh.

Later, Antoinette's grandmother said to her, "Your mother was right not to apologize. I would have apologized even if my cake were perfect. I wish I could be like your mom."

But it seemed to Antoinette that her grandmother did not want to be like her mother. Did she want to dress like her daughter-in-law, go to basketball games and listen to radio broadcasts of operas with her? Did she want to play tennis? No, Antoinette thought. Her grandmother didn't go into the exclusive shops on her own, not only because she felt too intimidated to go in, but because she knew there would be nothing in them that she'd want.

Her husband, when he came in, appeared worried. Antoinette was sure he thought his daughter-in-law was overexciting his wife. Antoinette could see fear in his eyes when he saw his wife wandering about, touching the edge of the table, the radiator, the doors, the walls. Then he stared at Antoinette, who was sitting silently at the table.

Antoinette thought about the small bungalow she was in, in which her father and uncles had been born and grew up, this rundown, little house with weeds growing in the yard and the pages of old newspapers always blown onto the porch steps from the street, and the sidewalk earth-trodden. It had to be the most rundown house in its part of the neighborhood, and Antoinette's mémère didn't seen to care that it was.

What, Antoinette wondered, was the Canuck secret? What was at the center of their souls that they really cared about? Was there anything?

Antoinette's mother didn't come again, and those things she had bought with Antoinette's grandmother for the house – place mats, a paper-napkin holder, a glass pitcher for milk – were used only for a short time, then disappeared.

At the end of the first year at college, Antoinette's mother asked her what her plans for the summer were. This was, Antoinette was sure, to let her know she should think of doing something other than spending the summer at the lake with her grandmother. But when Antoinette said she had a feeling her grandmother needed her, her mother said, "All right." At the lake house, she helped Antoinette unpack and put her clothes away in the small, slanting room under the roof, while her mémère sat on the bed and silently watched.

Her first evening after her mother left, Antoinette felt as if she had come to a convent in which she must take a vow of loneliness. When supper was finished her grandparents and her uncle Edmond went to their rooms. Antoinette went outside to sit in the warm, dark air. Soon, her mémère came out by the screen door and hesitated on the flagstone stoop as if she weren't sure why she'd come out, then she took a seat near Antoinette. Pépère came out, too; then, looking for them all, her uncle Edmond. Silent among themselves, they listened to the sounds of crickets and frogs, surrounded, these, by the sound of distant water lapping. The woods were filled with fireflies.

Her mémère didn't want to swim or lie on the blanket. For hours, Antoinette sat with her on the glider in the screened-in porch as Mémère rocked back and forth, back and forth, saying, "If I knew what I wanted."

Antoinette said, "I'll call Mom. I'll ask her to come. She will."

"No, no," her grandmother said, "no, don't. I don't want her to come."

"Why?"

"I want her to keep away from me. I don't want her to see me when I'm like this."

"She'll help you."

Stopping the glider with her foot, Antoinette's mémère said, "I don't know if I want her to help me."

Antoinette got up and went to her room. She thought, I've got to leave here. But after a while she thought she must go back to her grandmother. As she was going through the kitchen she stopped at the sink for a glass of water. Through the window above the sink, she saw her grandmother, down on the dock, looking at the lake. Antoinette saw, vividly, the spider webs on the outside of the window frame, the pine tree halfway down the slope to the lake, the listing, grey wood dock, the sunlight on the lake, even the small print on her grandmother's dress. Antoinette took a drink of water.

She went down to the dock. Her grandmother jumped a little when she approached her.

"Let me telephone Mom," Antoinette said.

"No."

Mémère has got to get away from here, Antoinette thought. She's got to.

In the autumn, her mémère went back to her house in the parish and Antoinette to a room at college.

Her mother met her in Boston, and Antoinette showed her around the city she believed was hers to show. It was a day when early snow was melting on the sidewalks, and her mother wore galoshes which were too big for her. Antoinette was at first anxious, because she wanted her to have a good time. Within minutes, she knew that her mother was having a good time, that she would have a good time anywhere. The sun was out. The shadows were clear. They walked along Commonwealth Avenue, Antoinette pointing out to her mother an iron fence, an old architrave, a gilt-framed picure seen through a window. Her mother would say, over and over, "Oo." They went into the Public Garden and stopped to look at the statue of Washington on his big horse. The air smelled of sea. Through the bare trees of the Common, to which they crossed from the Garden, Antoinette pointed out the gleaming gold dome of the State House. "Oo," her mother said.

Antoinette loved her mother for her love of the world, for her love of other people, for her love of streets and cars and shops and bars and churches and theaters and restaurants and houses, for her love of tables and chairs, of plates and cups and knives and forks, for beds and sheets and blankets and pillows. Though her world had no secrets – and, because no secrets, no possible meaning – it was what Antoinette wanted.

She told her mother she would, after she graduated from college, go away. She'd leave America. Her mother laughed.

Antoinette went home with her mother. She hadn't been home in what seemed a long time, and she was struck by the orderliness that she imagined was of the rooms themselves thinking themselves into order. Everything – lamp shades, bedspreads, rugs – was white, and seemed to think: space and clarity. Supper was almost formal, with white plates, crystal glasses, white cloth napkins. Antoinette wanted to talk about her mémère. She imagined Mémère standing outside, while they ate. They knew she was outside. How could they not refer to her? But no one did.

Finally, Antoinette said, "If only Mémère could get away."

Her mother said, "She's such a lovely woman."

"Yes," Antoinette said, "she is –"

"She loves her home."

Antoinette felt she could not go against what her mother said. "Yes," she said again.

"She –"

Daring herself, Antoinette interrupted. "No, she doesn't love her home."

Her mother smiled and tilted her head. "I think she's so lovely, if she were more so she'd be holy."

"No, she isn't."

Her mother sat back in her chair and looked away from her. "Phil," she said, "tell me about your work today."

He said, "I had a good day."

Antoinette went as often as possible by train to Providence. It was always a bad sign to find her mémère praying. When she was well, she didn't pray, and was, Antoinette thought, as indifferent to religion as she was to politics. Antoinette found her mémère sitting alone in the living room, her rosary of big, wooden beads wound around her wrist. Antoinette asked where her pépère was. "He went out," she said. Antoinette saw her look at the wrist wound round with the rosary, and she seemed to become embarrassed, for she covered the rosary with her other hand. Antoinette left her to go to her room because she thought she wanted to be alone to pray. And what did she pray for?

Antoinette had the fantasy, each time she left her mémère to return to college, of taking her off somewhere, to another country, where she'd help her out of her depression. Her mémère would become active and spirited and Antoinette would become active and spirited, too.

Alone in her college room, Antoinette thought about her mémère. She imagined her mémère split between believing she had to will herself to be better and believing, powerfully, that she must pray to God to be relieved of her will. But that was like wanting to die. And she wanted to live.

She said to her granddaughter, on Antoinette's next visit, "I don't want to die."

Antoinette hugged her closely.

More than ever, Antoinette wanted to talk to her mother about the cause of her grandmother's illness. However, she knew that her mother wouldn't talk.

Antoinette stayed at college for weekend after weekend to study, and then she went to stay with her mother and father. When Antoinette asked her father if he'd been to see his mother, her mother changed the subject before he could say yes or no. Antoinette realized that for her mother her grandmother had ceased to exist. And maybe her mother was right to consider that what was wrong with her mémère had nothing to do with the world. She was right to see her mother-in-law unwell as a non-person, someone who had no rights in society. And yet, this action made Antoinette angry, and she insisted on talking about her grandmother, not only in her mother's hearing, but to her mother. It was as if she herself weren't there, however, when she said to her mother, "I'm going to telephone mémère." While she was on the telephone, her mother went into another room, and Antoinette spoke in a loud voice. Her father shouted, "Can't you at least keep your voice down?" Antoinette raised it higher. Her father didn't shout again, which meant her mother was restraining him.

The next Saturday, Antoinette went to her grandmother's. She wandered listlessly around the small bungalow, wishing there were something else she could do besides trying to talk to her grandmother. Her grandmother's sadness palled on her. Her uncle Ed's story about devils appearing in the folds of a curtain in a house near the church palled on her. Antoinette left the same day.

She didn't go to see her mémère for she didn't know how long. She didn't go home either, but again stayed in her room over the weekends and tried to study.

I've got to be independent, she said to herself.

Her father telephoned her to say he was going to have to be in Boston for a day, and he wondered if she'd like to have supper with him after his meeting. Antoinette arrived at the restaurant before her father. Over the menu, she saw him open the glass door for her mother to go in ahead of him. Her mother smiled at her as she came towards her among the tables, at the centres of which were lit candles in yellow glass globes. Antoinette rose to hug and kiss her, then her father.

With her parents, Antoinette felt overcome by homesickness for the house she grew up in.

Towards the end of the meal, she said to her mother, "I've been thinking, you're right about mémère."

"What do you mean?"

Antoinette didn't explain. She said, "Look, why don't we go down to see her and convince her to come spend a few days at home? I could take a couple of days off from college for a long weekend. A change really would do her some good."

"She'd never leave her home," Antoinette's father said.

"She'd never come and stay with us," her mother said.

"Try," Antoinette said to her mother. "She'll listen to you, I think. If we could get her away from down there, just for a few days or so –"

"I'll try," her mother said to her.

"I feel you're saying that for my sake. Don't do it for my sake. Do it for Mémère's."

They found Antoinette's grandmother in the living room, in a big armchair, wearing men's dark glasses, though the blinds were all pulled down. Antoinette's mother didn't bring a gift, not even after-bath dusting powder.

Antoinette couldn't face her grandmother. She picked up an old magazine to look at the pictures.

She heard her mother say to her grandmother, "You've got to get out, just for a walk."

"Where can I go?"

Turned away from them both, Antoinette couldn't concentrate on the pictures.

Her grandmother said, "Tell me about the fruit trees in the valley and the fruit salad your mother makes, with all kinds of fruits."

But her mother raised her shoulders and asked, smiling, "Why can't you go anywhere you want? What's wrong?"

Antoinette looked up from her magazine.

"I know that your husband and sons love you," her mother said.

Her grandmother's face appeared to become small behind her large sunglasses.

Blushing a little, her mother asked, her chin out, "Didn't you want to get married?"

"Yes."

"Didn't you want children?"

"Yes, I did."

"Didn't you realize that if you had a family, you'd often have to do for your family what you didn't want to do?"

"Yes. I knew that."

"Then what is it?"

"I thought you would understand."

Antoinette's mother raised her chin higher. "Understand what?"

Her grandmother said, "Don't you know what?"

"Look, all I understand is that you should get away, at least for a while."

Antoinette's grandmother smiled at her mother. "No," she said, "I want to stay here."

Antoinette's mother got up and walked away.

And why don't I, Antoinette thought, why can't I walk away?

When her mother was leaving that Sunday afternoon, Antoinette thought she would insist that she come with her, but she kissed Antoinette and asked if she'd be getting a train to Boston later that day or in the morning. Antoinette said she'd stay the night with her mémère.

Her pépère went to bed early, her uncle Ed went out to the ice-cream parlor to see friends, and Antoinette and her mémère remained in the dim living room.

Her mémère's lips were pressed together with the determination to remain silent. It seemed to Antoinette that her mémère's body was itself aware of keeping her soul still. She was willing herself to be dark. Antoinette suddenly thought: I hate her. Antoinette's mémère had made up her mind to be as she now was, her lips tight, her jaw set, her eyes fixed on nowhere. She stared past Antoinette, but, at the same time, at her, able to convey that she was staring past her so as to cut her, or to cut herself away from her, from everyone. And the granddaughter stared right at her. It seemed to Antoinette they sat for hours. Then her mémère glanced at her, and Antoinette knew her will was broken.

Will-less, she gave in to something that surrounded, darkly, her will, something she must have known her family needed her to be aware of. Her family loved her, did love her, with all the pity and compassion in the world, for her darkness.

Antoinette got an early train to Boston, but though she was in time for a lecture she couldn't make herself go to it.

At the end of the week, she met her mother in a coffee shop in Back Bay. Her mother's chair was surrounded by shopping bags.

Lightly, as if touching on something that was taken for granted between them, she said to Antoinette, "Will you get a new dress for your sophomore dance?"

Antoinette said, "I haven't even thought about the dance."

She saw her mother's chin rise. "Please don't let your grandmother's sickness affect you in this way." Her mother said, "I wish I could stop you from going to her."

"Stop me? You wouldn't do that."

Her mother's smooth face became red with anger. "If I could, I would. When you had to obey me because you were younger, I should have stopped you."

Antoinette stood. She pushed her chair so it tipped towards the table and crashed against it, making the coffee cups tremble.

"Stop this," her mother said. "Stop it now, and sit back on that chair and finish drinking your coffee."

A relief, so sudden it made her feel weak, came over Antoinette, and she sat.

She didn't want to talk about her grandmother, but she said to her mother, "You don't understand her."

"What don't I understand?" The red face of Antoinette's mother was overcast with bewilderment. "Tell me."

"How can I tell you? It'd be like trying to tell you –" She stopped.

"What?"

Antoinette had never before thought that her mother understood so little; her mother seemed to her an innocent. "Never mind," she said.

"You understand," her mother said. "Tell me."

"Are you saying I understand because I'm like Mémère?" Antoinette said.

"Aren't you?"

Antoinette shook her head. "I'm not. I love her. But I'm not like her." Antoinette felt odd movements in her head.

"But you're not like me."

The movements in Antoinette's head felt as if parts of her skull were shifting about.

"You think I'm like Mémère?" she asked.

"Aren't you?"

"No."

They walked side by side to the exit of the coffee shop, Antoinette carrying some of her mother's shopping. It seemed to Antoinette that she had a big decision to make before they reached the door. As she held the door open for her she said to her mother, "Look, can I come back home with you for the weekend?"

"Well, that'd be nice," her mother said with a lilt. Antoinette didn't like that lilt. She thought her mother shouldn't feel happy that she wanted to go home.

On Sunday evening, her mother asked her, "Will you get the bus into Boston tonight, or wait till the morning?"

They were alone in the den, drinking white wine.

"I think I'll stay here for the week," Antoinette said.

Her mother frowned. "But your exams."

"I can do all the reading here. Honestly. Don't you want me to stay?"

"I want you to stay, yes –"

"I have the books with me that I need to read. I will read them, I promise. Honestly."

She did no reading. She stayed with her mother while her father was at work, and in the evening after dinner, when her father went down to his office in the basement, she and her mother sat in the den and drank wine and talked about the neighbors.

Wednesday evening, they went to a basketball game. Whenever her mother stood, Antoinette did the same.

Sometimes, standing by her mother, she looked at her shout out with her arms raised, and Antoinette smiled. She couldn't force herself to root.

In the car home, Antoinette said, "I should go see Mémère."

"But you're preparing for your exams."

"Yes," Antoinette said.

Antoinette thought her mother must be aware that she hadn't opened a book.

She and her mother, both on the big sofa with big cushions in the living room, listened to the radio. Her father was again working in his little wood-panelled office in the basement. Antoinette didn't know where her mother's interest in opera came from. Antoinette tried to be attentive. Her mother said, "Now this is when the heroine protests her helplessness," and Antoinette couldn't recall why the heroine should be doing that. Her mother, sitting up straight, closed her eyes. Antoinette slouched back a little and listened, and it seemed to her that all at once the singing wasn't emanating from the radio, but from herself. The music was lyrical and painful, and Antoinette thought she had never heard anything like it. Yet, she felt: I know this music. The song swelled out more and more the deeper the singer's voice went. Antoinette looked at her mother, whose face was expressionless. What does she understand of this music? Antoinette wondered. When the aria ended, her mother opened her eyes. She smiled a little in Antoinette's direction, but only for a moment before she closed her eyes again to listen.

Antoinette immediately thought of her grandmother.

At college, she forced herself to go to the lectures. She was majoring in economics. Her week's absence made the lectures difficult to connect with what she had learned, and she read to try to make the connections. Then when someone from the same floor knocked on the door and asked her if she'd like to go out for a beer, she said yes.

"I'll stay here this weekend," she told her mother over the telephone. "I've got to study."

"I only hope you're eating and sleeping enough."

Antoinette said, "Will you go see Mémère for me?"

Antoinette's mother came to her college room, which, Antoinette realized in her mother's presence, smelled of unwashed sheets. Standing at her desk, her mother opened the covers of books left there, then shut them. She looked back at Antoinette, sitting on her bed, and smiled, but she also frowned a little.

Trying to make her voice sound matter-of-fact, Antoinette asked her mother, "How is Mémère?"

"I don't know."

"You haven't seen her?"

"Not for a while."

Antoinette knew her mother wouldn't lie.

Antoinette picked up a magazine from the floor and asked, "Why?"

"I didn't think I would do her any good."

"Did you telephone her?"

"Of course I telephoned her."

Antoinette was folding back the corners of the magazine. "Did she say she wanted to see me?"

"I told her you were busy with your studies."

"I want to know if she said she wanted to see me."

"Well, yes, she did, of course she did."

Antoinette covered her face with her hands. "And was she better because I wasn't visiting her?"

"Mem was worse."

"Why?" She knew that this word was like a blank wall her mother could only stare at. "Why?" she asked again.

"I don't know," her mother said.

"You honestly think she doesn't have a reason to be the way she is, don't you? You honestly think she could change if she wanted to, if she just used a little will."

"I didn't say that."

"It's what you feel."

Her mother turned her face away.

"You won't recognize her world," Antoinette said, "You think it's just a backwoods world of people who're out of touch, who're certainly not Anglo-Saxons, and certainly not Protestants, and who maybe aren't even white."

"You said Mem hated her world," Antoinette's mother said, looking at her again. "You said Mem wanted to get out of it."

"Yes, yes, yes. As I do. As I do." Antoinette threw the magazine on the floor. "You were right," she said flatly. "I'm like Mémère."

"You can be what you want to be."

"Oh, if that were only so. You want me to believe that, but you know it isn't so. You said it: I'm like Mémère. You don't understand her world, but I do."

Her mother said, "I want to understand."

"You can't."

"You won't even try to tell me what I don't understand."

"No, I won't." Antoinette felt the words were being lifted from her on some dark voice she couldn't stop. "Because it's our secret. It's Mémère's secret, and mine, and we can't tell it."

"Your secret?" her mother said. "Your secret?"

Antoinette couldn't stop herself. "We know it, we know it, we know it –" Then, suddenly, she stopped, or the rising voice stopped. Tears were dripping from her jaw.

Her mother's eyes were on her.

Antoinette said, "I want to be like you, but you don't believe I can be like you."

Her mother leaned over her. "That's everything I want. That's –"

Antoinette wailed, "I understand Mémère's suffering."

"I'll tell your father if you don't stop. I haven't been

telling him about how you really are, as I've never really told him about you and your grandmother."

"Call him up. Call him up now. He understands, too."

The muscles of her mother's face were taut, and the tendons in her neck stood out. Antoinette saw that she knew that what she had said about her father was true. Her mother was beside herself. She clenched and unclenched her hands.

Antoinette said, "I'll leave college, I'll –"

"You can't leave college," her mother said.

"I haven't been able to study. I won't pass my exams."

Her mother hit one hand against the other. "You think you're stronger than I am, you and your grandmother. But you're wrong. You think you'll break my good will towards you by threatening to do everything you can to break it, like leave college –"

"I am leaving college."

"Then leave, leave and do whatever you want, but you can't break my good will towards you, you can't make me not want you to be a human being."

"How do you know that the only reason why you consider Mémère is not a human being, or I, or, for all I know, Dad, is because you expect from us what isn't in us? How do you know that, in her way, Mémère is human in terms you could never, ever understand?"

"Is she happy?" Antoinette's mother shouted.

"No. No. No."

Antoinette's mother sat by her. She held her hands out, her palms up. She said, "I am."

Antoinette threw herself against her mother, who, jolted, at first drew back, then put her arms around her daughter.

In her mother's arms, Antoinette felt a longing to see her grandmother that was so great it was as if her grandmother were dead and the longing were strong enough to bring her to life. Antoinette withdrew from her mother's arms. She stood. Her mother watched as she walked about the room, touching the edges of the furniture.

The longing to see her grandmother came over Antoinette with the deeper sense that if she didn't see her, she herself would die, because her grandmother kept alive in her what had most meaning to her.

Her mother thought that whatever there was between Antoinette and her grandmother was nothing that two people could share, or could even want to share, because it was inhuman.

Antoinette stopped in front of her mother. "I'd like to go see Mémère," she said.

She saw the disappointment in the face of her mother, who said, "Have I ever stopped you?"

"Will you come with me?"

The moment she said this, Antoinette realized she didn't want to go to her grandmother.

Antoinette's uncle Albert, who had been living in Hawaii as a retired Marine Corps major, was now living with his parents. He said flatly to Antoinette and her mother, "I'll stay with them till they die."

He cut the pie Antoinette's mother had brought at the kitchen table, around which his parents, his brother, his sister-in-law and niece were also sitting, and he served the slices on to the plates each one held up.

Eating her pie, Antoinette's grandmother said, "You're the best daughter-in-law the son of a mother could ever want."

Everyone looked at her.

The daughter-in-law tried to lower the level of praise to something like the truth by laughing and saying, "I don't think I'm really the best."

On the way home in the car, which her mother drove, Antoinette realized she felt worse than before the visit to her grandmother. She was frightened by this.

Calmly, her mother said, "When are exams?"

She was saying, she had done what Antoinette wanted of her, and she assumed Antoinette would do what was expected of her. She was saying she was doing everything she could, and the least Antoinette could do was the same. Antoinette began to sweat with fear.

Her mother, a careful driver, pulled out from behind the fast-moving car ahead and pressed the accelerator. The driver of the car accelerated, too, but Antoinette's mother drove even faster, until she was past the car, then she swerved in front of it. The driver flashed his headlights.

With a hard voice, Antoinette's mother said, "If you're not going back to college, you'll have to get a job. And you'll have to find yourself a room somewhere. Do you hear me?"

Antoinette heard herself say, "Yes."

Antoinette went to her room and fell half asleep. The door banged open against the wall and her father came in.

"What's this about college?" he said.

"I don't want to talk about it," she shouted.

"You're right. We're not going to talk about it. There's nothing to talk about. You're going to finish. After all the money I've paid out for you –"

Antoinette shouted more loudly, "Money!" She got up from the bed. "It's not the money. It's that you want me to do what you did."

"I don't know what you're talking about."

"You do know. You know what you did, and you want me to do the same, want me to go to college and –"

"Now you don't know what you're talking about."

"I do!"

The fight with her father was terrible. She kept expecting her mother to come in, as in the past, and stop it, but her mother stayed out. Antoinette picked up the lamp from her bedside table and threw it, lit, out into the room. The cord jerked it short, and it fell to the floor not far from her father and her; the porcelain base shattered, but the bulb remained lit. Antoinette's mother came in. She picked up the broken lamp, piece by piece, and switched the bulb off, then placed everything on the bedside table. Antoinette's father left the room.

"I can't take these fights between you and your father," Antoinette's mother said.

Antoinette looked down. "Dad refused to accept that I can't do –" She stopped.

"Of course he does."

Antoinette sat on the edge of her bed.

"Tell me what you can't do," her mother said.

Antoinette put her hands between her legs. She said, "You're right that nothing is stopping me from going back to college and taking my exams." She swallowed. She looked up at her mother. "Why am I like Mémère? I don't believe I've got Mémère's blood." Again she swallowed, but felt that whatever was in her throat wouldn't go down. "Why, though, am I like her?"

Her mother couldn't answer.

Antoinette said, "It's as if someone, some big dark woman, stepped into me –"

Her mother sat on the bed next to her. She brushed her face with her fingertips. She was, it seemed, trying to brush something away from her. "How did you think that?" she asked.

Antoinette shook her head.

"Listen," her mother said. "If you feel you can't get through to the end of college this year, I think you shouldn't be forced to. You can make up the semester next year. You need a change. Wouldn't you like to go stay in Texas with your grandma there?"

Choking on her sudden sobs, Antoinette said, "Let me go to Mémère."

Her mother drove her to Providence. Her grandmother, who didn't know they were coming, was frightened when she heard people come into the living room. From her chair, she said, "Who's there?" Antoinette's mother went to her quickly to say, "It's Jenny and Toinette," and she kissed her, but the look of fear stayed on Mémères face.

Antoinette's grandmother didn't ask her to come over to kiss her. Her mother sat close to her grandmother.

"Where's Pep?"

"He's sleeping. He's been sleeping a lot."

"And Ed and Albert?"

"They went up to the lake for the afternoon."

Antoinette went to the other end of the living room and looked out of the window at the weeds growing in the yard. She turned back into the room, in which old blankets hung over the armchairs and sofa. The room smelled shut in.

Her grandmother was hunched forward, trying to listen. Her black glasses kept slipping down her nose. She moved her lips as her daughter-in-law's lips moved. Antoinette thought that she and her mémère could not, in any way, be related. When she thought this, her grandmother, her glasses so far down her nose that her eyes were exposed, looked towards her.

"Antoinette?" her grandmother called.

Antoinette didn't move.

"Is that you?" her grandmother asked. "Antoinette?"

Her mother, too, turned to her.

Her grandmother pushed her glasses up over her eyes as Antoinette came towards her. Antoinette sat on a hassock at her feet. Her grandmother put her hand on her head, and she leaned forward so the glasses slipped down her nose again. Antoinette saw her grandmother look up from her to her mother. It was in her eyes that her daughter-in-law belonged to another world that had nothing to do with the world she and her granddaughter belonged to, because her daughter-in-law's world was without religion.

Quickly, Antoinette's mother said, "Mem –"

Antoinette's grandmother waited.

"Mem, I don't think Toinette should come down and see you again."

Antoinette shouted, "Ma." This jolted both her mother and her grandmother. "I'll see her, I'll see her," Antoinette said, "and no one, no one will keep me away from her."

Her mother said directly to her grandmother, as though

Antoinette had ceased to be there, "Mem, it's not good for her to be here."

Antoinette's grandmother asked, "Why?"

"Because every time she comes she loses more of her will, and she gains some other kind I don't understand. I don't know. I don't understand. But –" Antoinette's mother released her voice as if to sing out. "Please tell her not to come back."

The glasses fell to the floor.

"Please. Please tell her."

The eyes of Antoinette's grandmother crossed a little. She looked in all directions around the room. Frightened by her, Antoinette's mother stood. Antoinette stood, too, and she and her mother moved away from her grandmother, who seemed to have become blind. As though trying to see, she rose to her feet. She rocked back and forth. She shouted, in the voice of someone else, "Antoinette! Antoinette! Antoinette!"

Antoinette rushed to hold her grandmother.

Behind her back, she heard her mother say, her voice shrill with her terror, "Mem, let her go. Let her go. Please let her go."

Antoinette's grandmother didn't move.

When Antoinette let her go and turned, she saw her mother had left the room. Standing just outside the door to the living room was her pépère, an open newspaper hanging from one hand, looking in.

Antoinette knew she had done a bad thing. She should go after her mother, but she didn't go.

Just before final exams, which she knew she couldn't pass, Antoinette left college and returned home. Her father didn't speak to her. Her mother did, but only about cooking, plans for redecorating the house, the marriages and divorces of neighbors. Antoinette stayed in for a party her mother gave at about the time she, Antoinette, would have been taking her exams. Antoinette drank a lot at the party and heard herself laugh. In the morning, she went downstairs only when she knew her father had gone off to work, and she had breakfast with her mother, with whom she discussed the jobs she had interviews for. Her mother never mentioned college. She said, "The job at the bank sounds good, with interesting responsibilities." Antoinette drove off for her first interview, which was at eleven o'clock in Boston.

She waited in a small room with a translucent partition behind which she saw figures move. When she was called, she rose, it seemed to her, with pain, and during the interview, given by a woman with red fingernails and lips, she knew she wouldn't take the job, but would spend the summer with her grandmother. She didn't quite hear what the woman said at the end – perhaps that she would be contacted.

From a telephone booth, she called her mother. "Look, she said, "I'm taking the train to Providence to stay with Mémère."

"How did your interview go?" her mother asked.

"Please," Antoinette said, "please let me spend this summer with Mémère, this last one. I promise that in September I'll find a good job. I'll even go back to college and pay my way. Please let me do this."

She heard her mother breathing.

Antoinette pleaded, "I'll be all right, you'll see."

Her mother said, "I've always known you'd be all right."

This was the last summer Antoinette spent with her mémère, though most of the summer seemed to be spent looking for her mémère, who went off on her own. Often, Antoinette found her standing on the dock, looking down into the green water. Antoinette thought that to help her she must risk whatever it was that made her frightening. She herself did not seem to be frightened of anything. Antoinette made herself go to the dock. Her mémère didn't move, but Antoinette saw that she glanced at her.

She said, "Mémère."

Her grandmother looked into the water.

"Wouldn't you like to take a walk on the island?"

Her grandmother turned to her, her lips pressed together as if to keep her face expressionless, and Antoinette saw in her eyes a curious look, as if she recognized something she hadn't thought until that moment: that she had hurt her granddaughter.

She said quietly, "A walk?"

"I'd like it if you went onto the island with me."

Antoinette saw that look deepen in her eyes, the recognition of Antoinette suffering because of her.

"All right," she said.

Immediately, Antoinette knew her grandmother was agreeing for her sake. She didn't want that. Her mémère must come because she herself wanted to come, because she herself had this small desire, she who now had no desires. They crossed the broken bridge, Antoinette helping her grandmother across the gaps.

On the island, Antoinette picked a leaf of a plant with red berries and gave it to her mémère to taste for its flavor of mint; she pointed out from a distance the mushroom growing from the stump of a tree, then a red and black bird in the branches of a tree. Around them, as if stilled by the laurel bushes and the pine trees, the air smelled of water and resin. Antoinette said, "Look at this, Mémère, this is where a duck abandoned its nest," and she pushed back the branches of a bush to reveal, on the ground, bluish eggs amidst rotting weeds. "And in that tree a squirrel has its hole," she said, exaggerating her own interest, and aware, too, that she was being sentimental about ducks and squirrels, "Look. Look at this."

Silent, her mémère looked. Sometimes her mémère made the effort and said, "I see."

"Look at this, Mémère. Look at this."

"I see."

While Antoinette was searching for something else, her mémère walked away, along the path. Antoinette looked at the lake through the trees, then she went along the path. Her mémère was standing among pine trees.

Antoinette saw her as her dark mother, and she felt a moment of terror and great love, felt, together, that she must get her mémère away and that she wanted her to stay forever where she was.

That summer, Antoinette explored the woods on uninhabited shores. She went out in the old rowboat, into coves where no houses had been built. The waterlily pads slurred against the flat bottom of the boat, and so covered the surface that it was a surprise when the oars dipped into water below them and the prow left a watery path through them. Insects hovered low over the pads, and gathered in clusters on the lilies. The oars made loud noises in the locks, it seemed, as she approached the shore. She thought the sense she had approaching that unknown shore, alone, where the bushes were so thick she couldn't see an opening into land, was what any young person would have who imagined herself an explorer, but she swore that her sense was so particular it seemed not a fantasy but a recollection. She didn't believe in inheriting culture through blood, but when she let the oars slide down to the guards against the locks and drifted as she looked over the bushes into the woods where vines hung from the tall trees and birds caw-cawed from deeper within, her sense of approaching a place where no one had ever been was very keen, as if she were the first in all the world to approach a place unknown to the world, and she could not imagine where this sense was from. The smells of the woods came out to her as she drifted in. The boat softly hit the bottom of the cove. As there was no opening in the bushes, she stepped out into the warm mud and secured the boat with the stone anchor, which sank among large, slowly expanding bubbles. These bubbles rose about her feet, too, as she walked to the shore, where she parted the blackberry bushes to step on the damp, root-crossed ground.

After the death of her pépère, her mémère, for a brief period, was well, and then she got worse than she had ever been. Antoinette's uncles tried to take care of her in her home. They couldn't take care of her.

Antoinette couldn't keep up the job she had found in Boston. Her parents let her move back to their house. Her mother was natural towards her, her father formal, and she tried to stay away from him.

But she went with him the first time he visited his mother in the home that a social worker had found. It was a home where mostly Canucks went. Like her father, Antoinette talked, as if to keep her grandmother from talking. But her grandmother sat turned away from them, not, it appeared, listening. After a moment of silence, her father said to Antoinette that they should go.

On the way out, they spoke to a social worker who said it would take some time before Mrs Francoeur got used to being in the home.

Antoinette's mother had dinner prepared. During dinner, Antoinette tried to talk. Her father tried to talk. Her mother listened. The talk had nothing to do with her grandmother, or with Antoinette, either.

Her mother asked her if she was tired. Antoinette said, "Yes." She didn't look at her father. When her mother smiled with concern for her, Antoinette saw beyond her mother the white wall of the room, and it occurred to her that she believed in God. He offered only impossibility, the deepest impossibility of all being ever to understand him, but she believed in him, and she loved him, absolutely.

She helped her mother with the dishes, then, she said, "I'm going to have a bath and go to bed." While the bathtub filled with water, she undressed and with wads of cotton took off her make-up.

Part Three

&

ǝ

It wasn't true, Philip thought, that a man always marries his mother. His mother, at any time in her life, would have been incapable of giving a party.

The morning was still dark, but warm. In his pajamas, he went down to the kitchen. The wooden door to the outside was open, and through the screen door came the smell of the grass he had mown the evening before so the lawn would be flat for the tables and chairs. Under the glow of strip lighting beneath a kitchen cabinet, Jenny, at the counter, was mixing mayonnaise into a big plastic bowl of potato salad. She was in her nightgown.

He wanted to go back to bed with her. He looked into the bowl.

"We don't have a lot more to do," he said.

She laughed. "We've got so much to do."

After stretching out his arms to yawn, he lowered one, as if he'd planned just where, on to Jenny's shoulders. His pajama sleeve held to her nightgown. "We'd be able to do more," he said, "if we had another hour's sleep. We'd really be ready to work." When he rubbed his arm up and down against her, he felt there was only one thin, slipping layer of cloth between it and her bare back.

She licked her fingers and held them up and away from him as she turned round and pressed her forehead into his shoulder. "Just an hour," she said.

Again, she got up before he did. He lay in bed while she showered and he stayed in bed to watch her dress.

"Come on," she said. "Up. Up."

She was in dungarees and a cotton shirt.

In the dawn light, he started to dig a trench where there

were no trees overhead, near the tennis court. He was sweating when two neighbors, Bill and Tom, arrived with spades, having walked from their houses in the woods. Jenny brought them out cups of coffee on a tray. Philip continued to dig while Bill and Tom drank their coffee and chatted with Jenny, but they knew more than Philip about the whole business, and Bill said to him, "You're going too deep. You should start widening out now."

"Have some coffee," Jenny said to Philip and held the cup out to him.

He drank it at the edge of the trench as the neighbors dug.

"What can I do?" Jenny asked.

"You could collect dry branches to start a good, hot fire," Bill said.

"And we'll need some stones, about that big," Tom said to Philip, and held out his hands to support an invisible stone.

While Jenny, in the woods, was pulling out dry branches from the undergrowth and Philip, with a crowbar, levered stones out of the ground, a station wagon drove onto the lawn, and Bill and Tom went to help another neighbor, Ken, take out three bulging, dripping, burlap sacks. This was the seaweed. Next to the sacks on the ground, Ken threw down a folded tarpaulin. He drove the station wagon off the lawn.

The sun was up over the trees when the wives of the neighbors came in three separate cars, and they put the collapsible tables and chairs out on the lawn where Jenny asked them to, and covered them with paper table cloths which they held down with pebbles. There were ten tables.

While the men got the fire going to heat up the stones in the trench, a delivery van arrived. The four women, laughing, rolled an aluminium keg of beer across the lawn, their arms and legs flailing in all directions. Then with arms and legs still moving in all directions, so it was impossible to know how they did it, they hefted the keg onto a stump. The young delivery man was given a plastic cup of beer while the middle-aged husbands worked.

Jenny's voice was high. "Let's get this show on the road." Her laughter was high. She held up her cup of beer to the men around the fire which was burning in the long, wide trench. She put on being drunk, but Philip had never seen his wife drunk. The other wives followed her across the lawn and through the back door into the kitchen, all talking and laughing at a high pitch.

Philip looked through the flames at the stones. They were black on top, but in the spaces between them was a glistening whiteness, and it seemed to him he remembered staring at these stones before, and feeling, as he felt now, that he missed something.

"We'd better get some bigger pieces of wood on now," Bill said.

Philip's older, bachelor brothers, Albert and Edmond, arrived with their very old aunt Oenone, whose arms they supported as they walked her slowly to the nearest table, where she sat and silently drank beer. Colleagues from work and their wives came, some with grown up sons and daughters, and more neighbors. Then Philip's married brothers, Richard and André, came with their families. The long, curving drive down to the country road was filled with cars, and cars were parked on the road.

Philip stayed by the trench with the fire. He saw Antoinette in the crowd. With old brooms, he and Bill swept the embers away from the stones, glinting with heat, and Tom and Ken slit open bags of seaweed.

"Come on," Ken shouted out, "get the goods here."

And Jenny and the three wives ran into the house and out with the sacks, of lobsters and little neck clams and quahaugs which had been kept in the downstairs bathroom. While Tom and Ken pitchforked the seaweed onto the stones, the women, in clouds of steam, opened the sacks. Jenny ran back into the house for the burlap sack of partially shucked corn, which she half dragged along the grass until her brothers-in-law took it from her. Tom and

Ken were placing the lobsters and dumping out the clams on the hissing bed of seaweed, and the women were throwing onto it the corn from the bag; Philip and Bill stood to the side, each holding a corner of the soaked tarpaulin, and when all the food was out, these two, walking along opposite sides of the trench, drew the tarpaulin over, then sealed its edges with stones.

Jenny asked Philip, "Why didn't you tell me you were an Indian until after we got married?"

"I thought you'd worry we'd have papooses."

He caught himself looking for Antoinette.

His younger, bachelor brothers, Daniel and Julien, were coming across the back yard, and Philip went to meet them. He never asked his four bachelor brothers why they were not married. Daniel lived in London; Julien had picked him up at the airport. He and Philip embraced, then stood apart and looked at one another. Jenny rushed over and hugged him and kissed him on both cheeks, and Jenny and her brother-in-law laughed. She kissed Julien.

Daniel's other brothers called him, and he, raising his arms, went to them. On the way, Antoinette stopped him, kissed him and said, "You haven't forgotten, I'll be coming over some day," and she continued in another direction into the house. She stayed inside a long time.

When she came out, people had finished eating. She found her father at a table crowded round with neighbors, some sitting, and some, like him, standing. Ken's wife was talking. She was Russian. That is, she was born and brought up in Russia, but now she was an American. She was saying how interesting Russians would find a clam bake. The paper plates were filled with shells and cracked lobster claws and kernel-less cobs. Philip smiled at Antoinette. She said to Ken's wife, Tatiana, "I long to go to Russia."

Tatiana said to her, "It's a different country."

"I hope it is," Antoinette answered.

"Come on," Ken said to her, "this isn't such a bad country."

"I'm not saying that. And I'm not saying Russia is good. But it's got to be different."

Tatiana said, "Well, if I was born in America and had spent all my early years here, I'd want to go to Russia." She raised her hands. "Russia is the other country."

People were talking.

Philip said to Antoinette, "I'm glad you could make it." She was wearing a tee shirt and white shorts.

"Mom asked me to come, so I did for her."

"Well, I can't think of a better reason."

She smiled at him. "Would you like to have a game of tennis?"

"Later, maybe." Looking into his empty cup for a while, he said, "I guess I'll have a refill."

Instead, he went to find Jenny, who was at a table with his colleagues from work and their wives. They were laughing.

"What's up?" Philip asked.

"Bob here is telling us about the time you broke every single pencil on your desk," Jenny said.

Philip laughed.

"Sometimes," Bob said, "we think he's going to pick up one of us and break that person over his desk. He keeps us working right, Phil does."

Philip said, "My temper is exaggerated to give you all a bit of a stir. I'm really a mild, good-tempered man."

Everyone laughed.

Philip asked Jenny, "I wonder if you'd like a game of tennis."

She leaned far back in her chair and tilted it to see him. "So soon after eating?"

"A mild, good-tempered game," he said.

The court was surrounded by a high chainlink fence. He and Jenny often hit the net, but there was an ease to their swings which made them feel they were playing well. Through the fence, Philip saw some guests watching.

Going to pick up a ball near the net, Jenny stopped and,

bending forward, put her free hand to her side, just below her stomach.

Philip came round the net to her. "Has that pain come back?" he asked.

"I'd better stop," she said.

As they were leaving the court, he noticed that Antoinette was among the spectators. She took her mother's racket from her.

Albert called out to Jenny, "Come over here now and have a game of horseshoes with your brothers-in-law."

The unmarried brothers-in-law were pitching horseshoes by the woods.

"I'm pooped out and I've got to sit down," she called back. "I'm getting old."

Edmond shouted, "You? You'll never get old."

Antoinette said to her father, "How about some tennis with me?"

He didn't want to, but he said, "Sure."

Limbered up, he played well, but he felt the balls came from the air and not from anyone he knew on the other side of the net. It occurred to him, in his detachment, that Antoinette had become a kind of non-person to him, at best someone from some other country who was a foreigner in this one, and whom he wanted to remain a non-person, a foreigner. He didn't know why this had happened. They finished a set, and sweating, he said, "I think that's it for me." "Sure," she said. "I'll collect the balls," he said. "If you want," she answered. She left him on the court. Perhaps she too felt that they were too different from one another. He was strangely light-bodied.

His younger brothers, Daniel and Julien were the first to go. For others who wanted to leave also, there was a lot of backing down the drive to let out their cars. The relatives went, then the colleagues, but the neighbors, or some of them, stayed till the sun set. Jenny said to them, "You've got to stay till the beer keg's empty." The neighbors helped to clear up as they drank more beer. Philip knew that Antoinette had left, but he didn't know when.

When the last neighbors, Ken and Tatiana, left a cicada was still trilling in a tree lit by the lights from the house.

"We haven't finished the beer," Jenny said, turning the spigot so beer spurted out.

"Are you up to finishing it all now?"

She laughed. "We might try, just to see what'd happen."

Pressing a hand to her stomach, he asked, "How's the pain?"

"It's gone."

He wasn't drunk, he thought, but something had happened to him. They went into the house. The windows were open, and warm draughts sloughed through the screens. He had married Jenny because she was different from his family, and he had wanted to be like her. Now, perhaps, he could be like her. Where cross-currents blew together in the hallway, stirring fine hairs about her head, he put his arms around her. If it was false of him to imagine he could belong to the same bright country as Jenny, then he had to risk his falseness. He kissed her.

Jenny went into the local hospital, where she had given birth to Antoinette. As if waiting for her to give birth again, Philip walked around the waiting room. Whenever he sat to read an article in the newspaper, it seemed to him his sight kept slipping through the print. He was walking round when the family doctor came in and said the surgeon wanted to speak to him. The doctor didn't walk by his side, but ahead, and Philip followed him down a shiny corridor, past wheelchairs and stretchers on trolleys. The surgeon told Philip that Jenny had inoperable cancer of the liver.

Philip was aware that he got from his family, from his father especially, the feeling of intimidation, if not fear, that he felt towards people in authority. Philip remembered being in the back seat of the old family car when his father was called to the curb by a policeman for not stopping at a stop sign, and his father was too frightened to explain that he had in fact stopped, just where the policeman couldn't have seen him from around the corner, and he sat in silence while his licence was examined and in deeper silence as the policeman told him off, and then he said, "Thank you." It was as if the two doctors had arrested Jenny and passed sentence on her, and Philip, after a silence, said, "Thank you."

The doctor asked him if he wanted to see her.

"Can I?"

Hesitating at the doorway, he went in only when the doctor turned to him. Jenny was asleep.

He didn't want to telephone Antoinette. If he wanted to speak to anyone, he did not want it to be his daughter. At home, with a sense of giving in to something he knew he mustn't give in to, he dialled her number. The number had been written by Jenny on the first page of the address and telephone book which lay with old pencils and a screwdriver and elastic bands below the kitchen wall phone, and he dialled three times before letting it ring. No one answered. He called the hospital to ask if Jenny was awake yet and was told she would be asleep for hours. Then he wandered about the house. It was just as well he couldn't reach Antoinette, he thought, for he felt that talking to her was like some kind of sin. When he dialled her number again, and there was still no reply, he realized she must be at work. If he could think properly, he was sure there was one decision in all the confusion that was the right one. There was even a decision to be made about Jenny's illness; if he could order his mind he might, like a lawyer who knew how to appeal against a sentence, find it. He was sure it could be found. And he must do it on his own, without anyone's help. Certainly his daughter would not be a help. His daughter might make him feel helpless. But he must do something. Standing in the middle of his bedroom, he felt something in him give way. Just now, he thought, he'd do this: as it was already after three o'clock, he'd drive into Boston, which should take him over an hour, and wait on the sidewalk for Antoinette to come home from work.

He stood before the brownstone house, the stone crumbling at the cornices, where his daughter lived.

Striding among others along the sidewalk, she stopped and frowned when she saw him, then she drew her face taut against her frown and strode up to him.

"Hi," she said.

"I thought I'd come into town to see you."

In her room, he recognized some things from home, such as a lamp and a mirror, he hadn't noticed were missing. On the bedside table was a framed photograph of Jenny and him on their wedding day. He and his daughter stood at the foot of the bed.

He said, "Mom's dying."

As he said it, he felt that thrill through him which he suspected might have been the real reason he had come all the way to speak to his daughter. And he knew that Antoinette felt it at the same time. He knew by the way her facial muscles seemed for a second to flicker as if she were about to smile. Philip hated himself for coming. Antoinette made her face rigid.

"There's no hope?" she asked.

"No."

She said, "You know, the leaders of Russia are right to proclaim that being positive is a social duty."

"I guess that makes them heroic," Philip said.

"I know that if I were in Russia," she said, "I'd be put against a wall and shot. And they'd be right to do it."

Antoinette covered her breasts as if they were naked. Out of shame, her father turned away. When he turned back, he said with a hard voice:

"I came to warn you that we've got to do everything we can to help Mom."

"How can we?"

"We've got to make her feel absolutely certain that she'll recover."

"She doesn't know she won't?"

"I decided she shouldn't know."

"Is that right? Mom is the kind of woman –"

Philip stopped her. "It is right. I don't want her to even wonder if she's going to die. I want her to believe she's going to live."

Antoinette dropped her hands. As she stared at her father, her eyes widened and her lower lip stretched to reveal her bottom teeth. Philip stared at her severely. She pressed her lower lip tightly against her top lip, but her eyes remained wide.

Philip did not want to be false. He didn't ever want to be false. His jaw set, he waited for an impulse of belief that it was possible Jenny would live. It didn't come. He unclenched his jaw and said, "There is a possibility."

"You said –"

"Against everything I said, there is a possibility."

He was, he knew, like a party-line Communist Russian mouthing propaganda, and his daughter knew he was. All he could do was stand against his lying.

He said, "I'm sure we can help her recover completely."

Antoinette shook her head. She was weeping, and the tears spread across her cheeks. "I'm sure," she said.

"Now come home with me," he said.

She went to the hospital with her father, but she stayed in the waiting room. Philip knew she didn't want to see her mother. He, too, didn't want to see Jenny, and, again, hesitated at the door to her room. Jenny was awake. She was lying flat, and he had to sit on a chair by the bed and lean close to kiss her. Her face was pale. Her left arm, folded over the blanket, had a drip stuck in it.

"How do you feel?" he asked.

"Not much."

"Well, I guess you can't complain about that."

"They haven't told me anything." Her voice was low.

He leaned even closer to her. "It's pretty bad."

He touched his forehead to hers and closed his eyes.

"Am I going to die?" she asked.

His eyes open, he saw hers from so close he couldn't focus on them.

"No."

He sat back.

She blinked rapidly.

"You'll go to a special clinic in Boston," he said. "Is that all right with you?"

"Yes. Sure."

He said, "Antoinette's outside. She wanted me to see you first." He pressed his lips together for a moment. "She's come home to live."

Jenny continued to blink. She asked, "What about her job and her room and her car?"

"They'll hold till you get better."

"Shouldn't she be on her own, like the doctor said, helping herself?"

"I'll go get her."

Philip stayed in the waiting room. A drunken man was there, changing seats all the time. Philip stood at the doorway.

His father said he would never have an operation if he were found to have cancer. A cancer, his father had said, was a bear sleeping in you, and if you woke it up by cutting into it, it went wild. That image came from the Indians.

His father also said, *"Le cancer ne pardonne pas."*

A flat hatred for his parents came to him.

The drunken man put a hand on his shoulder, startling him, and asked Philip if he had a match. Philip said no, and felt badly for not having a match for the drunk.

You're not going to pull me down, he thought, imagining each parent grasping a hand as if to keep him from falling over as he stumbled through his baby steps. I'm not going to let you pull me down.

Antoinette came into the waiting room. She had a match for the drunk.

At home, she prepared supper.

They were silent at the table while they ate. Philip felt it was wrong to talk about Jenny, because talking about her, for whom there was no hope, had nothing to do with her, but only with Antoinette and him.

After dinner, in the den, Antoinette, as though she'd made up her mind to break the silence, said, "Don't you think it'd be a good idea to do a little redecorating while Mom's in the clinic, so that when she comes home she'll be surprised by new wallpaper and curtains?"

Philip made himself say, "I don't think it should be left as a surprise. I think we should ask her advice, and get samples of paper and swatches of material to show her."

Before she went to her room for the night, Antoinette said to her father, "You know, I really am convinced Mom will be back soon."

From the den, he watched her climb the stairs. He heard her slam her bedroom door, which she used to do when she was a girl.

Jenny was taken from the hospital to the clinic in Boston, and the first time Philip visited her he went alone.

He said to her, "Antoinette told me to tell you she thought we should be alone together." He laughed. "I don't know exactly what she thought we'd do."

Jenny, too, laughed.

"She's got all involved with the house," Philip said. "She wants it to be like new when you get back."

"I'm glad she's so involved."

"She's better than she's been since –"

"Since when?"

"I guess, since she was a little girl."

"That was a while ago."

"Maybe it just took her a long time to grow up," Philip said.

"Oh, I knew she would, finally."

He was glad Jenny didn't talk about her illness. He didn't want to talk about that.

"And what plans does she have?" Jenny asked.

"Beyond getting the house ready for you to come back to it, I don't know. She's so –" He couldn't think of a word.

"She's so anxious," he said, and thought, No, that's the wrong word, "for you to get better she can't consider anything else. I mean, she's anxious because she wants you to come back right away, doesn't want to wait."

"I'm happy her attitude's good."

"Her attitude is totally positive."

Jenny thought, then said, "Your mother's death was a big shock to her."

Though he didn't want to talk about this, he thought that to talk about it so openly, as openly as Jenny talked about everything, must be good, and he said, "A shock she needed."

"She loved your mother."

"Yes. But she's always loved you, too."

"I know that." She frowned.

Philip said, "You've become pensive."

Jenny's face, even her yellowish eyes, seemed to become clear, and she smiled.

"You always had faith in her," Philip said.

"As a mother, that's not so difficult."

"It goes deeper, it goes as deep as the deepest part of you, your faith in people. I know that, and Antoinette knows that."

Jenny kept smiling. Philip reached out and placed his hands on either side of her face and then leaned close and kissed her. The contact of his lips against hers sent a fine shock right down through him. He kissed her again, and when he sat back he crossed his legs and put his hands over his lap.

"Here we are talking about Antoinette," he said, "when she sent me alone so we'd talk about us."

He was sure Jenny knew why he had put his hands on his lap. Her smile widened. He blushed a little, but he thought what had happened was all right, and it was more than all right for her to know that she had made it happen. He smiled widely back at her.

He said softly, "I can hardly wait for you to get home."

"I can't be very attractive," she said. "I seem to get more and more sallow every day."

"No. In fact, you look better than when I last saw you in the hospital."

"Do I?"

He nodded.

She touched her fingers to her cheeks and looked into his face as though she were looking into a mirror.

He said, "You're so beautiful. I'm sure I've told you how beautiful you are, but if I haven't it's been because I'm shy. You're the most beautiful woman."

To hide her face, she spread out her fingers, but he saw her smile through them.

He said, "And I'm not just talking about beauty of character and all that. I'm talking about the way you look."

He saw, through her fingers, her smile narrow until her lips closed, and her eyes went as dark as the circles around them. He felt his pulse beat.

"I mean it," he said.

Quietly, she said, "I was just thinking you must be a little strange to find me so attractive now." She pushed back her nightgown and held up a grey-yellow arm to him.

"That's nothing," he said. "That'll go. Give it two weeks, and you'll be your old white again."

She stared at her arm, then at the back of her hand.

"Believe me," he said.

Shaking her sleeve down over her arm, she said to Philip, "You're right. But it'll take longer than a couple of weeks, I think."

On the highway out of Boston, he felt, for a moment, that his car was not going forwards, but backwards, and he was out of control.

"She's looking better," he told Antoinette.

"I've got ten samples of wallpaper for her to choose from for your bedroom," she said, "and twenty swatches of cloth for curtains."

"And have you talked to anyone about doing the work?" he asked.

"I thought we'd do it together," she said. "I'll do as much as I can when I'm not at the clinic with mom, then, when you have the time, you can help me do what I can't do alone."

He couldn't tell her he didn't like her enthusiasm. He had to say, "All right," trying to express his own enthusiasm at the lowest level, as if the more he kept it down the more convincing he might be. He said, "I'll do what I can."

Driving to work in the morning, he again had the sensation of suddenly going backwards. This frightened him.

As Philip was going to his desk, his friend Bob got up and met him.

"How is she?" Bob asked.

Philip said drily, "She feels it'll take longer, but my feeling is that she'll be home in a couple of weeks."

"That's great."

Philip was tired, and he didn't want to talk about his wife. He wanted to talk about work, which didn't make him tired. Maybe his colleagues thought he was inhuman, the way he kept his talk strictly to his work. His work did not require feeling, unless the feeling was of anger for something that didn't go well. But his anger might make his colleagues think he was even more inhuman. Then, he thought, let them think he was inhuman. Perhaps he was.

His company was designing and manufacturing lenses for the American military, to see the earth from space satellites, from which the earth could be destroyed.

Bob came to his desk in the afternoon. He said, "I don't know how we'll be ready for San Francisco."

"We will be ready," Philip said.

"If –"

Philip lowered his voice, but it was as if he raised it. "We'll be ready," he said.

It came so soon, the time when he had to leave to pick up Antoinette and drive into Boston. He took work with him, papers thrown onto the back seat of his car which, for security reasons, he should not have taken out of the company building. This was wrong, he knew, but that night he must finish work required by the colleague who was flying to San Francisco in two days. Antoinette was waiting in the drive.

He sat back while Antoinette and Jenny discussed the samples and swatches, and for a moment closed his eyes. He wished he didn't have to hear Antoinette's over-enthusiasm for the colors and patterns her mother liked best. When he opened his eyes he saw his daughter sitting on the edge of his wife's bed, both of them suddenly still. Next to his daughter, his wife looked thin and unwell. She saw him looking at her.

"You're tired," she said to him.

Jerking himself up, he said, "No, not really."

"I know how tiring it is to visit people in the hospital. I remember when you had to visit your mother."

"My mother was an entirely different case," he said, his voice sharp. "Entirely."

"It is tiring."

"Not to come see you." He made himself smile. "If I look tired, it's because of work."

"Tell me."

"It's too boring."

"You always tell me about problems at work."

"I will, I promise, when it gets really impossible. It's not that yet."

"You can tell Toinette. She'll listen."

"Of course," Antoinette said.

Philip said, "Show me what you've decided about the wallpaper and curtains."

After dinner, he told Antoinette he was sorry he couldn't help her scrape paper off the walls of the den. She said, "I'll do it." Philip went to his bedroom to work. He lay on the double bed, which Antoinette had made up with the white bedspread. He did not want to work. The papers were scattered over the bed, some on the floor, while he, propped up by pillows, wrote with a ballpoint pen on a pad of yellow, ruled paper. After a while, he thought: I can't do this. In his socks, he went down to the den, which Antoinette had emptied of furniture, and where, in a corner, she was scraping long strands of paper off a wall. The overhead light was dim, and bugs flew around it. Antoinette turned to her father when he entered the room, and didn't say anything, but looked around at the other walls. He wanted to say, You've taken on too big a job. He said nothing to her, but went back up to his bedroom. By one o'clock, he'd finished his work. Antoinette was still downstairs. He could hear her scraper against the plaster. Listening, he lay with his arms and legs spread out. Then he gathered all his papers together and left them on the bed to go downstairs and help a little. She had finished one wall.

In the morning, she prepared his breakfast.

"I'll go see Mom as soon as possible," she said, "and I'll spend all the time I can. I'm sure she wouldn't mind if you didn't make it to see her today."

"No," he said. "I'll go after work."

He got to work early, so that no one else would notice him come in with the papers he should not have taken out.

At his desk, he thought: Now use your will. But he thought this, he knew, against a longing to be will-less.

Antoinette went during the day to see Jenny; Philip went after work.

All the while he was with her, Philip kept thinking that his wife's life depended on his willing her to live.

She said, "But, look, I really am getting yellower." She was.

He said, "No, you're not."

"But I am."

Day by day, she appeared thinner and weaker, and one day he was startled to see how large her teeth appeared, how large her eyes.

What he must do, he thought, was to get her to think of

the world outside, and each time he went he tried to have news that would interest her about their neighbors, about their town, the state, the country, the whole planet, news that would make her eager to get out into the world again.

They walked up and down the clinic corridors. On the walls were stencilled notices about events: lectures, seminars, group therapy meetings.

Jenny said, "It's like being back at college."

"This time you'll graduate," Philip said.

"With what degree?"

He couldn't think of an answer that would keep the conversation going, and they walked in silence, she on his arm. He couldn't think of anything to tell her about the outside world. In her room, he said, "You'll be awarded the degree of Doctor of the Chin."

She stuck out her chin.

He found that after an hour with her a panic came over him, he did not know about what, and he had to leave.

He said, "I'll get back to Toinette and help her. The den's done, our bedroom's done, and we're now working on our bathroom."

"And the curtains are ready, too?"

"You'll be back before the curtains are ready."

"I wonder when I'll be back," she said.

He got angry. "You will be soon."

"All right."

"You know you will be."

"Please don't get angry."

This was the first time he could recall that she had said this, as though, having taken it for twenty-five years, she could no longer take his anger.

"I won't, if you don't make me angry," he said, and he tried to smile, but he felt his face become stiff.

"It's just that I've been here ten days," Jenny said, "and I don't think I'm getting better. Everyone here is geared into everyone getting better," she said, "so that you're never allowed to think for a second that you yourself might not be, but –" She shrugged.

Philip put his arms around her and hugged her. He felt her bones.

"If you want," he said, "I'll find out the official story – if that's any different from what's been told you, which I doubt – and I'll tell you honestly. Haven't I always told you the truth?"

"Yes."

"But I'm sure, I'm absolutely sure, of your recovery."

"Does it mean so much to you?" she asked quietly.

"How can you ask that? My life as it is depends on you. You know that."

Jenny held him close to her.

"And just think of what you mean to Antoinette. Just think of how you've helped her."

"I?"

"Yes, you."

"How have I done that?"

"By being what you are."

She pressed her head against his shoulder, pressed herself against him, as though to try to press herself into him and to walk out of the clinic in his body.

He said, "You know you've got your duty towards the world. You probably feel it's impossible, it's too demanding, the duty, now that you're weak. But I think it's just now that you should be most committed. I think it's now that you should make the biggest efforts to be –"

"What?"

He held her as closely as he could. He was frightened her bones would break. When he let her go, he felt that he let go of all sense of direction. He was not sure how he got out of the clinic, and, once in his car, in the floodlit parking lot, he did not know the way home. He sat for a while as if drunk, and, in his disorientation, he recalled a song from his college fraternity that made his eyes smart with tears for its inappropriateness now.

Show me the way to go home,
I'm tired and I want to go to bed.
I had a little drink about an hour ago
And it went right to my – cerebellum.

He had not even tried to find the doctors who knew what was happening to his wife.

On the freeway, where the New England woods crowded together beyond the lights, he could not remember which way he should go until an illuminated sign appeared to indicate it to him.

The wide freeway, lit up with glaring lights, made him feel entirely isolated in his car, and with the feeling of isolation came the vision of himself alone, driving forever on freeways at night, as though that was what his life was. And he also felt that he didn't have the right to drive, even in the slow lane, along these interstate highways, but felt they'd been made for the real countrymen, and not him. When he was driving with Jenny, he never had this feeling.

He thought: I'll work, I'll work as hard as I can, harder than I can.

His car, as he accelerated, seemed to him to go into reverse. He concentrated on the highway ahead, as if his concentration on what was ahead would keep the car going forward,

He must not say a prayer, because he knew that any prayer would work against what he wanted. For Philip, to pray was not to pray for willed brightness, in which nothing was promised, but for will-less darkness, in which alone there was promise. He didn't want what was promised. He hated it. He wanted to be in the soul-less world, and he wanted to be in it with Jenny. He wanted her to live.

Sweating, he willed the car to go forward. He had to think of every action, and told himself: Signal now to exit, shift into third gear, turn the steering wheel. As he drove along unlit country roads through woods, he kept talking to himself: Ahead is a fork, and you take the right, up the hill –

When he stopped at the top of the drive, he quickly shut off the engine. On, it could engage itself and send the car crashing into the woods. He sat for a while in the driver's seat, shivering with cold sweat.

He left the car in the drive and went into the house through the garage. As he opened the door to the hallway off the kitchen, he sensed that the house was empty, though the strip lighting was on under the kitchen cupboards and a light was on in the den beyond the kitchen. After he shut the door quietly, he stood still, waiting, it seemed, for something to occur that would let him know the house was empty. He took off his jacket and tie and put them over the back of a kitchen chair, then he pulled his sweat-wet shirt away from his body. He couldn't make himself call for Antoinette, and when he went into the den it wasn't, he thought, to look for her, but as if to check on the emptiness of the house.

He went up to his room and lay on the bed. Alone, he thought of himself without Jenny. He tried to stop these thoughts. His duty was to keep the image of her back home with him centered in his mind; when he lost the image, he imagined Jenny, too, might be lost. He often found himself wondering how he would keep the house in order, and whether his tax status would change so much he'd be unable to keep such a big house, or if he'd want to keep the house. Whenever he found himself thinking in this way, he'd fix his mind on Jenny again, until he would once more find himself thinking, not of her, but of himself alone.

When he thought of himself alone, he thought of his mother.

He could not imagine his mother united with his father in their deaths. He could only imagine her alone in her death, and, his arms and legs stretched out as if he had been knocked down – as a delayed reaction to the blow which had knocked him flat – he thought that it was all his fault, his mother being so alone. He turned over and pressed his face into the white bedspread. He could have saved her, could have had her come to live with him and Jenny. The guest bedroom could have been hers, and he would have taken her for rides in the car to see the countryside. And, further back, when he'd lived at home, he could have done more for her; he could have tried to understand her being isolated and maybe sometimes frightened by what her husband and sons wanted of her. And he thought, too, of what he could do for her now, as though there were still something to be done for her in her dark loneliness, if he had the real will to do it. He had caused his mother's death. He hoped his brothers never thought this.

He lay for a long while with his face pressed into the bed. He said to himself: Think of Jenny. He lay on his back.

In the silent room, he heard his mother call him.

His body was again covered with sweat. He got up and walked up and down his room.

What had he wanted of his mother, he thought, that caused her to die even before she died?

Come on, Jenny, he thought, calling her; come on.

What had he wanted his mother to be that he himself didn't want to be? What was it that made him marry someone so different that he would never even look for similarities in her with his mother?

Jenny, come on.

"Philip," he heard his mother say.

He went quickly out of the room and down the stairs. The wooden door to the outside was open, and Philip approached the screen door. In the light projected through the screen door he saw Antoinette. She was near what was left of the rotting stack of fire wood, and was looking away from the house. Her hands were to her face. A terror came over Philip. He stepped back noiselessly and went upstairs to his bedroom, where, breathing in spasms, he again lay on the bed.

Antoinette was in the kitchen when he came down. He startled her.

"I didn't know you were home," she said.

"I went upstairs to rest a minute."

"Supper'll be ready soon. Then you can go to bed."

"I feel all right just resting a minute."

"How was Mom this evening?"

Philip said, "I thought she was looking better. How did you find her today?"

"The same as you," Antoinette said, "better."

"I only wish she'd eat more. She's getting thin."

"That must be the food. Tomorrow, I'll go with her favorite meal."

"What's that?" Philip asked.

"Chicken and gravy and beaten biscuits. Didn't you know?"

Philip ran his hand over his face. "No, I didn't."

Antoinette turned away from him to a kitchen counter.

He said, "I was wondering –"

Turning back, she seemed to look around before she saw him.

"I was wondering," he said, "if we could go to see Mom together. I'll take off from work, so I can go during the day with you. And I'd like it if you came with me in the evening."

Again, she appeared to look around the room before she said to him, "I'll do whatever you want me to do."

When he sat with his wife and daughter, he listened to them talk. They always found something to talk about. And yet, he didn't feel there was a special relationship between them; he felt that it was ordinary, as their talk was ordinary. It was he who had a special relationship with his daughter.

Jenny's eyes stared from her grey-yellow face.

She said, "When I'm better, first thing I'm going to go stay with my mom and dad."

"I'll tell them that," Philip said. "They'll be very happy."

"Now grandma will start decorating their house," Antoinette said.

"Why don't you telephone her?" Philip said. "Tell her now."

"I've been making a lot of calls to her," Jenny said.

"Go ahead," Antoinette said. "Call her."

"I'll do it," Philip said.

From her room, he dialled and spoke to his mother-in-law in Texas in a voice he knew was too loud, as if her distance from him required his almost shouting; but he was talking so loudly because he was excited, though he did not know about what. He handed the receiver to Jenny.

She said "I'm planning on coming home soon."

Driving home, Philip sensed in Antoinette's silence that she wanted to talk. He didn't want to talk. He knew what she would say: that they should be truthful. He wanted to be truthful, especially, he felt, to his daughter. But why, he asked himself, why should the truth always be to state what was impossible, why never to state what was possible? A fine thrill went through him, as of something finally and totally completed. Then he told himself, No. No. We don't die.

After they ate, Antoinette said to her father, "The new curtains arrived today."

Her father said, "I'll put them up."

"Now?"

"Yes, now."

Her eyes filled with tears. "I'll help you."

"You rest."

"I'll help you," she said.

All the while she and her father inserted the little hooks into the tops of the curtains, tears ran down her face, so she had often to wipe them with a tissue which she then screwed into a wet ball and put beside her on the armchair. Philip didn't say anything to indicate he saw her tears. He asked her to hand a curtain up to him when he got on a ladder before the wide window of the living room.

She held it while he hooked it onto the rod, and she continued to weep, sniffing her tears and mucus back into her sinuses and wiping her eyes from time to time with one hand. Her father said to her only, "You can let go now." Philip went for the next curtain. Antoinette held it as he hooked it up, though it was not necessary for her to hold it. They collected together the wrapping paper and string from the floor.

Philip wanted to comfort his daughter, but he couldn't. He couldn't embrace his daughter and kiss her forehead, couldn't touch her.

After she had spent two weeks in the clinic, Philip was told that Jenny was expected to die in another two weeks.

He said, "I'd like to have her come home."

That evening, he and Antoinette sat in the den and ate take-away food from paper plates, which she cleared away. He kept to his armchair, his face turned away from the room, and when she took her place again on the end of the sofa, she looked at the floor.

As if to someone not present, he said, "Why do I feel, when I'm told that there's nothing to be done, Well, that's what I thought all along?" His voice was dry and low.

"Dad?" Antoinette said.

He looked at her.

"I didn't hear what you were saying," she said.

He sighed deeply, and the sigh seemed to cause a spasm in his lungs. "Oh, Antoinette."

"Yes."

"I was just thinking –" He stopped. "I was just wondering –" Those spasmodic sighs stopped him from talking. "Why, all my life, have I wanted people to fail?" He stopped for a long while. "In school, I wanted my classmates to fail, and didn't like them to get even passing marks. And I was the head of the class." He stopped and put his hand to his forehead, concentrating on his breathing. "In college it was the same, and in the Air Force. I was always at the top, and I wanted everyone else to fail, but really fail, not just do worse than I did. At work, I'm glad when one of my colleagues botches up a job, even though it's against the interests of the company. I'm glad when we don't get the contract we were counting on, so we begin to wonder if the company will go under. It's strange. I've always been that way."

Antoinette said, "If I said I know what you mean –"

"I know that you know what I mean." His breath heaved. "But we can't let Mom die." His breath heaved more.

"Dad."

"We –" His breath broke.

Antoinette went to him. She tried to put her arms around him, but to do that she had to take an awkward position on her knees, her body twisted in his lap.

Jenny arrived the next morning in an ambulance. She was able to walk around the house and didn't want to stay in bed. With Antoinette's help, she changed her nightgown for a dress. She was thin and weak, and the grey-yellow of her face and hands was deepening.

She was asleep in what was now only her bedroom when Philip came home from work, and while he and Antoinette ate in the dining room they spoke in whispers in case their voices woke her.

Philip asked, "How was she today?"

Antoinette simply put both hands over her mouth and stared at her father.

"Did she show any interest in the house?"

Lowering her hands, Antoinette said, simply, "No."

"Maybe, her first day, she was too tired."

"Maybe."

Philip saw on his daughter's face that, seeing her mother at home, she had accepted that she would die. He didn't want to stay with his daughter. He didn't want to try to make her lie by saying she believed his wife would live. After he finished eating, she said she'd clear and wash the dishes, and he said he'd go prepare the guest room for himself.

The small room was under a gable, and hot. He opened the window. By the time he had made the bed and hung up in the closet the clothes he needed, it was dark, and he lit the bedside lamp.

He imagined the house below him, the cellar, the kitchen and dining room, the living room and den, the bedroom his wife was in, the bedroom his daughter was in, and the attic gables above him.

He wondered if saying a prayer for the house and everyone in the house would change the way things were. He wanted to make an appeal. He could so easily find himself appealing to the world he was born and brought up in to have him back, if, in fact, he had left it; to have him and his daughter and his wife, as if in that world it was possible to withdraw from the present world, where whatever was promised had to be fulfilled by determination, to the past world, where whatever was promised was beyond him or anyone to fulfil, and was fulfilled of itself.

His window was open, and insects with pale wings and antennae and long, articulated legs were whirling on the outside of the screen, attracted by his bedside lamp. He switched the lamp off.

When he did, the house seemed to him to become a place he didn't know, and he couldn't say where it was and what he was doing in it.

As tired as he was, he wouldn't, even if it were possible, appeal to his past world. He did not want to go back there.

It came to him that his mother had hated the past world as much as he did, that she'd longed to get out of it as much as he did.

That's over, he thought. That world is gone.

He would lie, he would lie and lie, if he had to, about there even being another world to belong to. His belief that it wasn't too late for his mother any more than for his wife was as false as any belief could be. But he had that belief. He insisted on it, with all his will.

Though it wasn't late, he thought he'd go to bed, and he undressed slowly.

In bed, he closed his eyes, and a vision came to him of his mother and wife. He couldn't hear what they were saying, but they were talking a lot, and they laughed. They were sitting across from one another at a table, cups of tea between them. There was a white cloth on the table, and the cups were white. The walls were white and bright, as the large house they were in was white and bright. His mother laughed and she put her hands to her mouth. His wife smiled at his mother laughing. His wife and his mother were at peace, they were happy. He believed this for them.

Most of the time, Jenny stayed in her room. Philip and Antoinette didn't go in when they knew she was on her knees by the bed, praying.

A hot evening, Philip and Antoinette were in the den. All the windows were open. Philip was the first to see Jenny come in, and he stood. Antoinette stood.

"We thought you were asleep," she said.

Jenny said, "I woke up." Her bones showed. She sat, and the others sat. In a little girl's voice, she said, "I'm going to live."

Part Four

&

As Antoinette was following her father up the cement stoop, she dropped her keyring. Her father was at the door, a brown door with a small-paned window in it; the door was being opened for him by a man whose white face Antoinette saw through the window. She picked up her keyring and called, "Dad" and he stopped and turned round to her. Her father came down the long stoop to her.

She said, "I can't go in."

His jaw tightened. She wondered if he was going to be angry with her. His eyes moved as he looked at her.

It seemed to her that her life in the world depended on her not going into that funeral parlor where her mother was laid out.

Her father's eyes went still on her. The door of the funeral home remained open, the face behind the window looking out. Antoinette leaned against her father and he put his arms around her shoulders and held her. When she drew back, she saw the lashes of his narrowed eyes were wet. His voice low, he said, "You'd better go before anyone else comes. Go to Boston, go shopping or to a show or –" He reached into his pocket for his billfold, from which he took some bills. "Take these," he said, "and –"

"No."

"Yes," he said, "take them, and for God's sake –" Here he lost control of his voice.

She took the money in one hand and her keyring in the other she held her father's head and kissed his eyes.

"Go on," he said, "go."

Beyond him, she saw the door to the funeral home open more, and her fear, of nothing more than that the man behind the door would appear on the top step, made her quake; she was about to fall, but her father held her arm.

"Are you sure you shouldn't just go home?" he said.

"I wish you and I could go home."

"We will."

She watched her father go into the funeral home and the door close behind him. Her father, she thought, was going in to face what no human being should ever be required to face. Her impulse was to go after him, to pull him back. She was trembling, and she realized her fear was not caused by what she would see if she went into the funeral parlor – what her father was now seeing – but by her desire to go in and see her mother dead, her desire to witness what she believed no human should ever see. She wanted to kiss her mother's dead face, but she could not allow herself to want that. Her mother would have told her to go, go right away, from such a feeling. Her mother would have told her not to go into the funeral parlor. Her mother would have said, "Go away, go away."

In her car, parked under a maple tree, Antoinette sat until she stopped trembling. In the meantime, she saw, at a distance, her uncles get out of cars and go up the stoop into the funeral home.

Uncoordinated, Antoinette had to think carefully of what she was doing when she started the car and drove out from the shade of the maple trees, then through the town that, on this summer morning, was familiar and entirely unfamiliar. She had never before been aware of the shadows of the maple trees.

Boston wasn't where she wanted to go, not, certainly, for shopping, which she could not have forced herself to do. She'd go to her old room.

A green and white interstate sign indicated an exit to Providence. About to pass the exit, she swerved without signalling, out from the wrong lane, and the car behind her blared its horn. The exit took her to a highway south.

She wanted to pray, but the only place where it was possible for her to pray was in the parish church of Notre

Dame de Lourdes. The church was brick, on the top of a hill, and its steeple was crisscrossed by electricity and telephone wires. Inside, there was no one. The linoleum tiles down the main aisle gleamed with wax and led to the altar rail, beyond which, as her eyes weren't yet used to the dimness, she saw only the red sacristy light. She walked to the altar rail, along it, and to a side altar with a statue of Our Lady of Lourdes, then up the side aisle. She stopped before the confessional at the back of the church. This was where her father had gone to confession when he was a student at the parish grammar school; in front of the statue of Notre Dame de Lourdes he'd said his penance and promised not to sin again. But the moment she thought this, she thought she couldn't see her father in this church as a little boy.

She sat in a pew in the Canuck church.

Her father understood why she wasn't able to see her mother dead, because he felt the same as she. But he didn't have a choice, he had to go into the funeral parlor and see –

Antoinette checked that thought by wondering how much choice her father had had in his life. She wondered if he'd had the choice of believing in his wife or believing in his mother. She though that her father must have been more divided than she in not knowing which country he was a native of, as if belonging were a matter of choice.

She thought about her mother as she imagined her father thought about her. She felt the loss as she knew he felt it. And she thought about how her father felt the loss of her grandmother. She wanted to pray for him.

She knew that nothing she prayed for would be granted, though. She had to pray, if she were going to pray, to a God who promised nothing. This church was the church of such a God, and she believed in him, because all Antoinette could believe in was impossibility.

Maybe, she thought, he wasn't a God, but the dead, or a God made up of all the dead, who were around this world in a world that was different from this, but who, from that different world, looked at the people in the living world, and sometimes, for a moment, appeared to them.

This was not a religious belief she had, Antoinette thought, as it offered no consolation, but she knew it was not invented by anyone – it existed in itself, like weather. It was a belief as true as weather, as true as death.

Antoinette wept.

In her car, she drove around the old parish with its poles at street corners and wires strung out in all directions. It was hot, and the air smelled of melting tar. Only because of her father, she thought, had she ever been interested in this parish. Only because of him had she wanted to go to his church, stand in the asphalted playground of his school, look into the stores where he bought comic books. But now she could not see her father on these streets, among people in shorts and checkered trousers and sundresses, walking past the shops with aluminium fronts.

Antoinette still had a key to her father's childhood house. She parked her car under the maple tree outside the back door. The rooms were dusty and airless, but they were as she remembered them. In the bedrooms the beds were made and the venetian blinds were shut. Antoinette looked in all the rooms, then in drawers and closets.

She went up into the stifling attic and, sweating, looked through cardboard boxes. She realized she was trying to find the old cardboard box that contained her father's belongings from the time when he considered this house his home. She remembered that box and some of its contents; she wanted to look at those contents again. In one box, she found pieces of old dresses, in another skates. Many boxes contained textbooks. She couldn't find the box her father had stored away. Hardly able to breathe, she went back down to the cooler, dim rooms.

She could not imagine her father here. The furniture looked old, the carpets worn. There was a water-mark on the living room ceiling, and a crack in the plaster wall of the kitchen.

On the way back up north, Antoinette went a little out

of her way to take the familiar road which led to the house on the lake. As she drove along the dirt road, people on garden chairs under trees or sunning themselves by the water looked up to see who was passing. The house was at the end of the road. She didn't have a key for it, but walked round it. The blinds were drawn so she couldn't see in. On the cement floor of the screened-in porch was an old magazine. She didn't mind that she didn't have a key; she didn't want to go into the house. Looking up at its timber eaves, she wondered why she had come. This house seemed to have nothing to do with her father's, or even her, past.

She turned away from the lake, from the sounds of motor boats and people shouting, and walked slowly up into the woods behind the house. There were tin cans and old bicycle tires and rusted automobile parts on the ground among the trees. It seemed to her she had once been able to go so deep into the woods she didn't see or hear anything outside them; now, she never lost sight of the roof of a cabin, and she heard a radio. The afternoon sun was lengthening through the trees.

An hour later she was in her room in Boston. She thought she should go back to her father, but she didn't know what to say to him. She would have to talk to him in a way she never had before. How could she?

Her window gave onto a fire escape and the branches of a ginkgo tree. She sat in front of it. The room darkened.

She wanted to tell her father something that neither he nor she had ever thought.

The light above the garage of her father's house was lit, and cast shadows of trees down the drive. In her car, Antoinette watched the shadows of leaves move across the hood.

At far distances crickets were trilling, but just around her was silence, and she walked, it seemed to her, in that immediate silence up the path to the back door of the house. From further away than the crickets, she heard children shouting. High above the dark trees the sky was still light. She climbed the seps to the wooden porch. Through the screen door she saw into the kitchen. His back to her, her father was at a kitchen counter. He appeared to be leaning against it. The lighting under the cupboards illuminated a loaf of bread whose wrapping was torn open, a half-empty bottle of milk, a carton of eggs with broken shells by it, a bunched up dish towel, tea mugs, old newspapers. The kitchen floor was dirty.

He turned to her when she opened the screen door.

"I was making something to eat," he said.

"Then I'm just in time." She looked round him at the bowl of eggs he was beating.

In a quiet voice, he said, "I can add a couple more eggs to this if you're hungry."

"I'll do it for you."

"I'm all right."

"Let me do something," Antoinette said.

"You could make toast, if you want."

She had the toast cut into buttered triangles for her father to spread the scrambled eggs over them.

She went ahead of him into the dining room with place-mats and napkins and cutlery to set the table, and he followed with the plates. He sat, but before eating he waited for her to go out to the kitchen for two glasses of milk.

"What did you buy in Boston?" he asked.

"I didn't buy anything."

"I was hoping you'd come back with a dress to show me."

"I went to Providence," she said.

He quickly looked away, then looked back at his plate and ate.

"I didn't use any of the money you gave me," she said.

"Keep it."

"No," she said. "When I show you a new dress, it'll be one I bought with money I earned."

He looked up at her.

"Sometime soon, I've got to get back to work," she said.

"Yes," he said.

"I want to get back to college."

"Yes, you've got to, and I'll help you if you need money for that."

"I'd like to try to do it myself."

Her father looked down again at his plate.

He finished eating, and Antoinette said to him, "You go into the den. I'll clear the table."

She also cleared up the kitchen, and washed the floor with a sponge mop.

When she went to her father in the den, she said, "Come on, let's take a walk."

"I don't know if I'm up to it," he said.

"A short walk to the quarry and back, then we'll go to sleep."

The night was hot and calm. Along the country road, the street lights lit up insects that flew out of and into the woods. There were crickets in the old stone wall that separated the road from the woods.

Through trees, Antoinette saw the light of a fire, and then, as she and her father got nearer to the quarry, she saw the flames of the fire, and heard loud splashes of water amidst the shouts of boys and girls. She knew from when she was a teenager what was happening. The quarry was just off the road; a fire was burning near it. While others looked, a teenager was diving from a ledge into the quarry pond, in which couples were swimming in firelit water. Antoinette stood with her father on the road and watched.

The next morning, she stood by her father at her mother's burial. Her father touched the metallic, shining coffin, then she did.

After, her uncles and aunts and cousins, and her great aunt Oenone, came to her father's house, but they didn't stay. Her father embraced his brothers, holding each in his arms for a long time, before they left.

For her father, Antoinette cleared her mother's drawers and wardrobe and closet of her clothes and shoes, and packed them in old suitcases and boxes. In the bathroom, she put into a box her mother's brushes and combs and her make-up, most of it unused. She didn't know what to do with the suitcases and boxes, but didn't want to ask her father, so she piled them up in the storage space beneath the rafters of a gable, to which there was a small door at the back of her mother's closet. In the bedroom, she changed the sheets and pillowcases on the bed, the old sheets and pillowcases her mother had slept in until she had been taken to the hospital four days before. Antoinette brought them down to the laundry room in the basement, next to her father's office, where, with his door closed, he now was. She heard the air conditioner from behind the plywood sheets and joists of the walls of his office. Back in the bedroom, she cleaned the wooden floor with a dust mop and the surfaces of the furniture with a rag. She left the photographs, some in frames and some in clear plastic cubes, of her mother and father and herself at different ages on the top of the chest of drawers.

Her father came up from the basement when she was getting lunch ready for them.

She said, "You can move back into your room."

He turned a little away from her, then said, "I'll stay in the small room where I've been sleeping."

Antoinette hugged him closely.

He said, "Don't go back to Boston for a while."

In the afternoon, they again took a walk. There was no one at the quarry. They walked around the quarry pool, then up a path into the thin woods and down the other side back to the road.

Antoinette said in a low voice, "Mémère and Pépère didn't know when their ancestors came to America, did they?"

"No," her father said, and shook his head a little. She didn't know if this was because he couldn't talk more, or didn't want to.

David Plante was born in Rhode Island in 1940. He is the author of several novels, including the Francoeur Family trilogy, *The Foreigner*, and *The Catholic.* He has also published one work of nonfiction, *Difficult Women.* In 1985 he was Writer in Residence at King's College, Cambridge. A regular contributor to *The New Yorker,* he lives in London.